PUFFIN CLASSICS

MYTHS OF THE NORSEMEN

ROGER LANCELYN GREEN (1918–87) became interested in myths and legends at an early age. His boyhood schooling was interrupted by bouts of illness, which kept him at home in Poulton Hall, Cheshire, where he browsed continually in the magnificent Queen Anne library. Andrew Lang's fairy-tales, H. Rider Haggard's adventure stories, traditional legends from around the world – these were his early influences.

Perhaps most significant is the influence of Andrew Lang, the Victorian compiler and presenter of fairy stories, myths and legends. When Green was at Oxford he made a special study of Lang; later he became particularly well known for pursuing the same literary course as Lang, as a presenter of traditional stories.

Writing was not, however, his first or only job. He had been a stage actor (especially as Noodler the pirate in *Peter Pan*) and schoolmaster as well as Deputy Librarian of his old college at Oxford. But from 1946 onwards, a large number of books appeared – biographies of his favourite authors, original children's fiction, and some fifteen volumes of his own retellings of traditional stories. Several of these retellings – the present volume included – are acknowledged to have attained the status of classics.

So here is Yggdrasill the World Tree; here are Odin and Thor, Freya and Loki. If these names are at all familiar to the English-speaking world, it is scarcely an exaggeration to say that this is due to Green's work in this volume, which was first published in 1960. For he brings to the stories in this volume not just his gifts as a story-teller, but also his particular ability to bring sense and clarity to a formerly confusing and scattered mass of legend.

Some other Puffin Classics to enjoy

THE THREE MUSKETEERS
Alexandre Dumas

MOONFLEET
J. Meade Falkner

THE ADVENTURES OF ROBIN HOOD
KING ARTHUR AND HIS KNIGHTS OF THE ROUND
TABLE
THE LUCK OF TROY
THE TALE OF TROY
TALES OF ANCIENT EGYPT
TALES OF THE GREEK HEROES
Roger Lancelyn Green

ALLAN QUATERMAIN
KING SOLOMON'S MINES
H. Rider Haggard

THE PRISONER OF ZENDA
Anthony Hope

ROGER LANCELYN GREEN

Myths of the Norsemen

Retold from the Old Norse
Poems and Tales

Legends that once were told or sung
In many a smoky fireside nook
Of Iceland, in the ancient day
By wandering Saga-man or Scald
Longfellow

Illustrated by

ALAN LANGFORD

PUFFIN BOOKS

PUFFIN BOOKS

Published by the Penguin Group
Penguin Books Ltd, 27 Wrights Lane, London W8 5TZ, England
Penguin Books USA Inc., 375 Hudson Street, New York, New York 10014, USA
Penguin Books Australia Ltd, Ringwood, Victoria, Australia
Penguin Books Canada Ltd, 10 Alcorn Avenue, Toronto, Ontario, Canada M4V 3B2
Penguin Books (NZ) Ltd, 182–190 Wairau Road, Auckland 10, New Zealand

Penguin Books Ltd, Registered Offices: Harmondsworth, Middlesex, England

First published as *The Saga of Asgard* 1960
Reprinted under the present title 1970
Reissued in this edition 1994
3 5 7 9 10 8 6 4 2

Filmset by Datix International, Bungay, Suffolk
Printed in England by Clays Ltd, St Ives plc
Set in 12/15 pt Monophoto Plantin

Dedicated to
The Masters and Boys of
Dane Court, Pyrford, Surrey
my own contemporaries and
those of my sons

CONTENTS

AUTHOR'S NOTE

'This is the great story of the North, which should be to all our race what the Tale of Troy was to the Greeks.'

WILLIAM MORRIS

This book is an attempt to present the surviving myths of the Norsemen as a single narrative, from the making of the world to the vision of Ragnarok. Into the framework of the *Volo-spa*, the finest of all the poems of *The Elder Edda* and one of the oldest, I have fitted the myths contained in the rest of the ancient Norse poems, and the prose tales collected by Snorri in the two books usually known as *The Prose Edda*. Many of the poems have found their way into my text in almost literal translation, and much of Snorri's narrative; gaps have been filled from Saga fragments – notably in Chapter 10 which follows *The Volsunga Saga* where Snorri's synopsis is inadequate. In the stories of Odin's wooing of Rinda and the two voyages of Thorkill the Wanderer, the rationalized versions given by Saxo Grammaticus have been restored to their mythological state, since no earlier authority survives. Scraps of ballad and folk-tale have helped to fill in small gaps – though

I have been forced to skate over one or two, such as Loki's introduction to Asgard, on the thinnest of evidence.

Norse mythology is the very antithesis of Greek from the reteller's point of view. The wealth of literature and legend available for studying the gods of Olympus is positively embarrassing, and the problem there is one of selection. The gods of Asgard, on the other hand, remain strangely aloof: the difficulty here is to find enough about them. And when the scanty material is collected, it is still harder to fit together the incomplete jigsaw-puzzle which is all that remains to us.

Most previous retellers of the Norse myths have contented themselves with a selection of isolated stories – or else have tended to exceed the licence of invention which a reteller should be allowed. Even that classic version *The Heroes of Asgard* by Annie and Eliza Keary, written just over a hundred years ago (1857), spreads a gentle and romantic glamour over the stories there woven together which opens the magic casements on a very misty view of the Nine Worlds of Norse mythology and the deeds wrought in them.

Of course any version of old myths, legends, or fairy-tales must reflect the outlook of the teller of these tales – and doubtless *Myths of the Norsemen* is as 'dated' as any.

I have, however, tried to the best of my ability to keep to the spirit of the original, that air of 'Northernness' which is so apparent even in

Vigfusson and Powell's literal translations in their *Corpus Poeticum Boreale* of all the surviving poems. I have tried to vary the poetic quality of the *Volo-spa* with the folk-tale quality of Heimdall's visit to Midgard or Odin's rough and ready dealings with the Giants when intent on stealing the magic Mead, or the burlesque quality of some of Thor's adventures, with the fate-ridden saga of Sigurd and Brynhild and the sheer epic of Baldur's fate – one of the great tragic stories of the world.

To mould all these together into one narrative, always following my originals closely, has been an interesting experiment, and one worth making. For the great Norwegian and Icelandic Sagas of the deeds of real or half-legendary men and women were woven much in this way, and out of just such diverse material – strung together often on the thin thread of a single family's history.

The Sagas of Midgard, whether the heroes be Gunnar or Grettir, or Sigurd himself, all end in tragedy – in the picture of the brave man struggling in vain against the powers of fate – 'And how can man die better than facing fearful odds?' This was the Norseman's view of life – and the deeds and fate of the heroes of saga must have been but the earthly counterpart of the deeds of the Gods of Asgard in their struggle against the Giant forces of nature so apparent to the men of the North, and of the doom, the Ragnarok, which was to overtake them.

With this view in mind I have tried to tell the

tale of Asgard and the Æsir – *The Saga of Asgard*, though in this new edition I have called it *Myths of the Norsemen*, since my original title was found to be too obscure.

THE ÆSIR AND THE GIANTS

'GINNUNGAGAP'

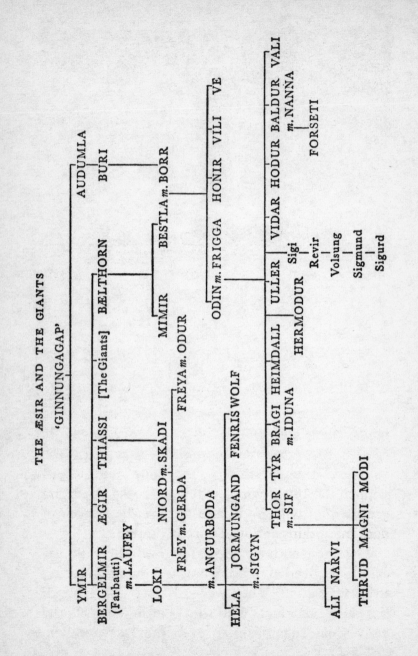

YGGDRASILL THE WORLD TREE

In the northern lands the summer is short and the winter long and cold. Life is a continual battle against the grim powers of nature: against the cold and the darkness – the snow and ice of winter, the bitter winds, the bare rocks where no green thing will grow, and against the terrors of dark mountains and wolf-haunted ravines.

The men and women who lived there in the early days needed to be strong and much-enduring to survive at all. They were tillers of the ground, but also warriors who did battle against the wolves, and against men even more savage who came down from the mountains or up from the deep sounds or fiords of the sea to burn their homes and steal away their treasures and their food, and often their wives and daughters as well.

Even when there were no wild beasts and wilder men to fight, it seemed that the very elements were giants who fought against them with wind, frost, and snow as weapons. It was a cruel world, offering little to hope for; yet there was love, and honour, courage and endurance. There were mighty deeds to be done and bards or skalds to sing of them, so that the names of the heroes did not die.

And, just as the deeds of men were remembered in song and story, tales were told of the gods, the Æsir, who must surely have fought even greater battles in the beginning of time against those Giants of Ice and Frost and Snow and Water who were still only kept at bay with difficulty.

In the very beginning of time, so the Norsemen believed, there was no Earth as we know it now: there was only Ginnungagap, the Yawning Void. In this moved strange mists which at length drew apart leaving an even deeper Gap, with Muspelheim, the Land of Fire, to the south of it, and Nifelheim, the Land of Mist, to the north of it.

Surtur the Demon of Fire sat at the world's southern end with his flaming sword, waiting for the Day of Doom, to go forth and destroy both gods and men.

Deep down in Ginnungagap lay the Well of

Life, Hvergelmir, from which flowed rivers which the cruel breath of the north froze into grinding blocks of ice.

As the ages passed the grinding ice piled up mysteriously above the Well of Life and became Ymir, the greatest of all Giants, father of the terrible Frost Giants, and of all the Giant kin.

Ymir grew into life, and with him appeared the magic cow Audumla whose milk was his food. And very soon the ice of Ymir broke off in small pieces and each became a Rime Giant – a father of witches and warlocks, of ogres and trolls.

Audumla herself needed food, and she licked the ice about her and found in it the salt of life that welled up from Hvergelmir.

On the first day that she licked the ice there came forth in the evening the hair of a man; the second day she licked, and in the evening there was a man's head showing; and by the ending of the third day the whole man was there.

He was the first of the Æsir, and his name was Buri; he was tall and strong, and very fair to see. His son was called Borr, and this Borr married the giantess Bestla, and they were the mother and father of the Æsir who planted the World Tree, Yggdrasill, and made the Earth.

Borr had three sons called Odin, Vili, and Ve, and of these Odin, the Allfather, was the greatest and the most noble.

They fought against Ymir the great Ice Giant, and slew him, and the icy water gushed from his wounds and drowned most of the Rime Giants, except for one who was named Bergelmir. He was wise and clever, and for this reason Odin spared him.

For Bergelmir built himself a boat with a roof, and took shelter in it with his wife and children so that they escaped being drowned in the flood.

But Odin and his brothers thrust the dead Ymir down into the void of Ginnungagap and made of his body the world we live in. His ice-blood became the sea and the rivers; his flesh became the dry land and his bones the mountains, while the gravel and stones were his teeth.

Odin and his children set the sea in a ring round about the earth, and the World Tree, the Ash Yggdrasill, grew up to hold it in place, to overshadow it with its mighty branches, and to support the sky which was the ice-blue skulltop of Ymir.

They gathered the sparks that flew out of Muspelheim and made stars of them. They brought molten gold from the realm of Surtur, the Fire Demon, and fashioned the glorious Sun Chariot, drawn by the Horses Early-waker and Allstrong, with the fair maiden, Sol, to drive it on its course. Before her went the bright boy, Mani, driving the Moon Chariot drawn by the horse All-swift.

The Sun and Moon move quickly, never pausing to rest. They dare not stop, even for a moment, for each of them is pursued through the day by a fierce wolf panting to devour them – and that fate will befall them on the day of the Last Great Battle. These two wolves are the children of evil, for their mother was a wicked witch who lived in the Forest of Ironwood: her husband was a giant, and her children were werewolves and trolls.

When Odin had set the stars in their courses and had lit the earth with the Sun and Moon, he turned back to the new world which he had made. Already the Giants and other creatures of evil were stirring against him, so he took more of the bones of Ymir and spread the mountains as a wall against Giantland, or Jotunheim. Then he turned back to the land made for men, which he called Midgard or Middle Earth, and began to make it fruitful and fair to see.

Out of Ymir's curly hair he formed the trees, from his eyebrows the grass and flowers, and he set clouds to float in the sky above and sprinkle the earth with gentle showers.

Then for the making of Mankind, the Allfather Odin took an ash tree and an elder upon the seashore and fashioned from them Ask and Embla, the first Man and the first Woman. Odin gave them souls, and his brother Vili gave them the power of thought and feeling, while Ve gave them speech, hearing and sight.

From these two came children enough to people Midgard: but sin and sorrow overtook them, for the Giants and other creatures of evil took on the shapes of men and women, and married with them, despite all that Odin could do.

The Dwarfs also had a hand in this for they taught men to love gold, and of the power that comes with riches. They were the little people who lived in Nifelheim, the region of mist, and in great caves under the earth. They had been made out of the dead flesh of Ymir, and the Æsir gave them the shape of men but a far greater cleverness in the arts and crafts of working with iron and gold and precious stones.

These Dwarfs, with Durin as their king, made rings and swords and priceless treasures, and mined gold out of the earth for the Æsir's use.

For after Midgard was made, wise Odin turned to the shaping of Asgard, his own strong and beautiful land, high in the branches of Yggdrasill the World Tree. The first palace was all of shining gold, and it was called Gladsheim, the Place of Joy: there Odin sat on his high seat, with beautiful Frigga his queen beside him.

Next they made palaces for their children, the great gods and goddesses who were so soon to play their part in the long struggle against the Powers of Evil: for Thor the Lord of Thunder and his wife Sif of the golden hair; for brave Tyr the young and battle-eager, guardian of the gods; for bright Baldur, fairest of all the Æsir, and sweet Nanna his wife; for Bragi and Iduna, who delighted in music and youth; for Uller of the Bow, and Vidar the Silent, and many another.

Round about Asgard stood great walls and towers, halls and palaces; and in the middle was the fair plain of Ida, where grew gardens of delight in front of Odin's palace of Gladsheim.

Every day Odin and the Æsir rode forth over the Bridge Bifrost, which appears to men on earth as the rainbow, and went down to the Well of Urd beneath one root of the Ash Yggdrasill – all, that is, except mighty Thor who dared not tread on that delicate arc for fear his weight might break it. He had instead to go round by the rough road over the mountains, and the Giants ran in terror whenever they saw him coming. Bifrost Bridge glows in the sky, for at its foot burns a bright fire to prevent the Giant kind from crossing it and so reaching Asgard.

Down in the shady gloom at the foot of the World Tree the Æsir held their council, to decide how they might bring help to mankind, and what must be done in the long war against the Giants. Down there under the Ash, beside the Well, stood a fair hall where dwelt the Norns, the three weird sisters Urd, Verlandi, and Skuld, who knew more even than Odin himself. For Urd could see all that had chanced in the past, while Verlandi had the power of knowing what was being done in all the worlds at the present; but Skuld was the wisest of all, for she could see into the future – and that not even Odin himself could do.

Often in time to come the Norns appeared at the birth of a hero to spin his web of fate and give him gifts of good and evil that should determine his future life.

They could tell Odin of the course of the world, and from them he knew, as well as from his own wisdom, of Ragnarok, the Last Great Battle, which must come at the end of the world when the Æsir and their Giant foes would fight out to the bitter end the great contest between Good and Evil.

The Norns also tended the Ash Yggdrasill, and watered the greatest of its roots daily from the Well of Urd. For the evil ones strove continually to destroy the World Tree: down in Nifelheim, where one root grew, the evil Nid Hog was for ever gnawing at it, while serpents twined and bit. Higher up four harts ran upon its branches and nibbled at the leaves, while at the top sat a wise eagle watching all that was done, and Ratatosk the mischievous red squirrel scampered up and down it, carrying news and gossip between Nid Hog and the Eagle.

In the midst of this strange and complicated world sat Odin the Allfather, like a kindly spider, in the centre of his web. His seat, high above Asgard, was called Lidskialf or Heaven's Crag, and there he sat and surveyed the world, with his two tame ravens Hugin and Munin perched on his shoulders. To them he owed much of his knowledge, for day by day they would fly forth throughout the world and return in the evening to tell what they had seen: Hugin, swift as thought, and Munin, unrivalled for memory.

Odin looked forth and saw how the Giants

plotted evil behind their high mountains in Jotun-heim. He looked towards Midgard, and saw how the race of men toiled in their fields, with scarce a thought of war and battle-glory, and he felt that more must yet be done and speedily – so that there might be warriors to stand beside him on the day of the Last Great Battle against the Giants.

So he called to him his son Heimdall, the White God, who had been born mysteriously in the morning of time, and who had nine mothers, wave-maidens from the world's end. His teeth were of pure gold, and he could see as well by night as by day. Indeed his sight was so keen that he could see things a hundred miles away; and his ears were so sharp that he could hear the grass growing in the earth and the wool on the backs of the sheep. Odin had made Heimdall the Watch-man of the Gods with a dwelling-place on the brink of Asgard beside Bifrost, with the great Giallar Horn beside him to blow if the Giants attacked Asgard – a horn that could be heard in all the worlds.

'Heimdall, my son,' said Odin, 'go forth into Midgard, taking upon you what disguise seems good. Go among the men who dwell there: good and simple people they are, but not yet to my purpose. Choose among them those who are most deserving, and see to it by the magic arts which are yours that from them come the three orders of mankind – so that ever afterwards a man shall be born with those gifts which he can best use in his life, to do excellently that for which he was made, and not as now to do many things but none of them well. Let them be doers, makers, or leaders in due numbers – born each to play his part – so that a mighty race may arise from which I may draw those Heroes of Midgard who shall stand beside us at Ragnarok.'

So Heimdall disguised himself as a sturdy wayfarer and went over Bifrost Bridge and down on to the Middle Earth, where he strode gaily along the green paths through the woods and fields until in the evening he came to a house.

The door was ajar, and in he walked. On the hearth a fire burned, and a pot hung over it, and on either side sat the master and mistress of the house, the peasant Ai and his wife Edda in her hood of coarse home-woven cloth.

'Welcome, stranger,' they said. 'Tell us how you are named, and then make yourself at home.'

'I am Rig the Walker,' Heimdall answered, and he sat down on the middle seat with his host and hostess on either side of him.

Then Edda broke the loaf, heavy and thick and mixed with bran, which was their usual supper, and served it to the guest with broth from the pot.

When darkness came Rig the Walker did indeed make himself at home. For he lay down in the middle of the bed where it was warmest and softest, while Ai and Edda were forced to lie on either edge.

Three nights the strange guest lodged there, and then he went on his way, smiling to himself.

But nine months later Ai and Edda had a son whose name was Thrall. He grew quickly and became a strong and sturdy man, with hard hands and thick fingers, broad back, long feet, and ugly face. He married a wandering girl who came across the moorlands with bare feet and sunburnt arms, and they had children who built fences and tilled the fields, tended pigs and herded goats and dug peat for fires. Their sons had names like Clumsy and Clod and Lout, while their daughters were called Cloggie, or Cinders or Lumpy-leggie.

Meanwhile Heimdall went on his way through Midgard, and on the next evening he came to another house. The door was on the latch, and he walked boldly in – to find a fire burning on the hearth and the good folk sitting there busy at their work. They were called Gaffer and Gammar, and were well-dressed and tidy – he with his beard trimmed and his hair cut, and she with a clean smock and a kerchief round her neck.

'Welcome, stranger,' they said. 'Tell us how you are named, and then make yourself at home.'

'I am Rig the Walker,' was the answer, and he sat down on the middle seat with his host and hostess on either side of him.

Then Gaffer served the supper of savoury soup followed by boiled veal, and afterwards showed their guest to the one bed of the house. There Rig the Walker did indeed make himself at home. For he lay down in the middle of the bed, with his host and hostess on either side to keep him warm.

Three nights Rig the Walker lodged with Gaffer and Gammar, and then he went on his way smiling to himself.

But nine months later a son was born to Gaffer and Gammar. He was called Karl the Craftsman, and he grew up a sturdy, ruddy-cheeked, laughing man. He was skilled at training oxen to pull the plough, at building houses, at smithying and making carts and ploughs. When the time came they found a wife for Karl the Craftsman, and the pair kept house together, farmed their land, wove their own linen and saved their money carefully. They lived happily and their sons bore such names as Yeoman, Farmer, Smith, and Neighbour, while their daughters were called Housewife, Spinster, Lassie, or Milkmaid.

Meanwhile, however, Heimdall continued on his way through Midgard, and on the next evening he came to a great house with its doors towards the south. In he went, for the bars were not down, and he found there two goodly folk dressed in fine clothes who could look him straight in the eyes when they spoke to him, and whose hands were long and white and shapely. Their names were Squire and Lady, and he was busy twisting a bow-string and setting it on his long-bow of elm-wood.

'Welcome, stranger,' they said. 'Tell us how you are named, and then make yourself at home.'

'I am Rig the Walker,' came the reply, and he sat himself down on the middle seat with his host and hostess on either side of him.

Then Lady spread an embroidered cloth of fine linen and set upon it loaves of white wheaten bread, well-cured ham and roast poultry on silver dishes, wine in a tall jug and silver-mounted beakers.

After the meal they sat and talked over their wine until it was bedtime. Then Rig the Walker did indeed make himself at home, for he rose first from the table and lay down in the middle of the bed, so that Squire and Lady must needs lie on either side of him.

Three nights Rig the Walker stayed with Squire and Lady, and then he went on his way smiling to himself.

But nine months later the son of the house was born, with yellow hair and rosy cheeks and eyes as keen as an eagle's. His name was Warrior Lord, and as he grew up his skill was in bending the bow, hurling the javelin, riding on horseback, sword-fighting, and swimming.

When the boy was on the verge of manhood Rig the Walker came again out of the dark forest, to teach him further skills, and to show him his place in the world.

'You are Lord of the Lands of Udal,' he said, 'and they shall belong to your sons and your sons' sons for ever. For I am one of the Æsir who sit in Asgard, and I declare you my godson, and give you this lordship, and make you a ruler of men.'

Then Rig the Walker, who in Asgard was Heimdall the Bright One, taught Warrior Lord much wisdom, and led him to high adventures in Mirk Wood, the dark forest where trolls lurked. He showed him how to brandish his sword, shake his shield, and gallop into battle.

And Warrior Lord gathered fighting men about him and took lands from those evil men who sided with the Giants. He married Princess, and their son became the first king in Midgard, a King of Denmark. This king gathered his lords and warriors together and conquered the land and gave it peace.

After that he feasted his people in his great hall and gave gifts of golden rings to those who had fought most bravely. Thereafter they practised much with their swords, and rode their horses, and went forth to give battle against any who would have invaded their lands or done harm to their people. But the king learnt wisdom as well as valour, and knew something of the mysteries of life and of the will of Odin.

For Heimdall told his godson of the great war between the Æsir and the Giants, and of Ragnarok, the battle that was to be. He told him how Odin had decreed that all who fell fighting bravely in battle were to be brought after their death to Asgard to form the army of the Æsir which should fight on that last day.

For when Heimdall had returned to Asgard, before Warrior Lord was born, he had found a new palace standing beside the Field of Light. This was Odin's great hall of Valhalla with its five hundred and forty doors through which eight hundred warriors could pass at a time. Its roof was tiled with shields and the rafters were the shafts of spears. The pillar which held up the centre was a mighty living tree; its leaves fed the magic goat Heidrun who gave in place of milk an endless stream of mead, the sweet beer which the Heroes were to drink.

When there were Heroes ready to fall in battle, Odin sent out his Valkyries to choose the bravest of them for his never-ending banquet. These Valkyries, the Maidens of Odin, the Choosers of the Slain, were immortal women – some were Odin's own daughters – who would ride through the clouds behind him when his hunt was out. At other times they flew about the world in the likeness of swans, to see who was fittest to sit in Valhalla. Sometimes they walked the earth for a while, letting fall their swan-cloaks, and bathing in solitary pools or rivers. If any man found them thus, and hid away their cloaks, the Valkyries seemed no different from mortal women, and could be wooed and wedded – as certain of the Heroes of Midgard were to find. But any Valkyrie who married a man of Midgard became from that moment an ordinary mortal woman.

Sometimes as Odin rode on his hunt strange things would chance. One night when the storm-winds raged and the thunder roared over the mountains, Olaf the Smith crouched over his fire in his smithy in Heligoland and prayed that no evil might befall him.

Suddenly he heard horse's hooves clatter on the rocks outside, and a heavy knock sounded on the door.

Trembling, he rose and opened it, and there stood a mighty king dressed in gleaming black armour with a broad sword at his side. He was leading a great horse which snorted and neighed impatiently, pawing the ground and shaking its bridle.

'Open quickly, master smith!' cried the King. 'My horse has cast a shoe, and I have far to ride before the break of day!'

'Whither are you going, noble sir, in such haste and so late on such a night?' asked Olaf the smith as he led the great horse into the smithy and examined its hoof.

'The night is clear and I have no time to lose,' answered the King. 'I must be in Norway before day dawns!'

'If you had wings, I might believe those words!' replied the smith, laughing at what he took to be a joke.

'My horse is swifter than the wind,' came the answer, 'and the wind will reach Norway more swiftly than bird can fly. But the stars pale: make haste, master smith.'

With trembling hands Olaf chose out his largest horseshoe and tried it on the hoof which rested on his knee. The curved iron was far too small: but as it touched the hoof it began to grow until it fitted into place. Filled with awe, the smith drove in the squared nails and marvelled to see the points rivet and buckle themselves down without his aid.

'Good night, Olaf the smith!' cried the king, as he leapt upon the horse's back. 'Well have you shod Odin's steed! And now to the battle!'

Then, as Olaf knelt on the ground looking after him, Odin galloped away into the clouds, a light shining round his head – and once more the hunt went thundering by as he sped on his way to a great battle after which many a Hero would be chosen by the Valkyries.

So the numbers grew in Valhalla, brave men and mighty warriors who sat every night at the banquet board. The mead flowed freely, but however drunk they were, there was never a headache amongst them in the morning. When day came they would arm, and go out into Odin's Field amongst the golden trees and there fight each other to the death, yet rise unharmed and return to Valhalla in the evening in perfect friendship.

While they fought, Andhrimnir the cook killed the great boar Saehrimnir and broiled his flesh in a gigantic kettle. Yet Saehrimnir was always alive again next morning, ready to be killed and eaten again that night.

Then the Heroes would sit down at the banquet

board to feast on the boiled pork and the plentiful mead, while the minstrel of Asgard sang stirring tales of the beginnings of things – of the war between the Æsir and Giants, and perhaps of the battle that was to be when the day of Ragnarok should dawn.

2

ODIN IN SEARCH OF WISDOM

There were many Heroes now in Valhalla, but it
seemed to Odin as he sat aloft on Lidskialf that
the years must be many before the Valkyries could
choose a great enough band of warriors to be of
use at Ragnarok: and would the Giants wait? That
he could not learn; as yet the Norns would not tell
him, if even they knew.

Odin therefore decided that he must seek all the
means of wisdom which he could find, that by
knowledge and by guile he might keep back his
enemies until his Heroes were ready for the Last
Battle.

Many and strange were the ways in which he sought for wisdom. He sought it even among the Giants themselves, going to Jotunheim in disguise to learn from the son of the Ice King.

He sought also for the wisdom of the dead, and hung for nine nights and days on the gallows – sacrificed to himself. For he caused himself to be hanged from the branches of Yggdrasill the World Tree, and gave command to the Æsir that none of them should give him bread or wine during that time. And thus the mysteries of death were borne up to him from the depths below the Nid Hog's den, before he came down from the tree.

After this he visited the Dwarfs in their caverns beneath the earth, and learned what he could of their special knowledge from Dvalin, wisest of them all.

Lastly he made his way down to the very roots of Yggdrasill, and following that root which stretches out towards the land of the Rime Giants, the children of Bergelmir, he found the wise Mimir. This was the brother of the friendly Giant-ess Bestla who was Odin's mother, and he was the wisest of all living creatures. Down there in the ultimate depths of the earth he guarded the very Fountain of Wisdom, and himself drew from it each day one precious draught.

'Wise Mimir, give me but one horn of water from your well,' begged Odin.

'Not so,' answered the Giant, 'for I may not part with my treasure lightly – not to anyone who will not give his most precious possession in exchange for that draught of wisdom.'

'Now, by Asgard the Blessed!' cried Odin, 'I would even tear one eye out of my head if it would buy me the right to drink of this water and acquire such depths of wisdom that I might thereby save those who dwell in Asgard and in Midgard!'

'That is indeed the price of the draught of wisdom from my well,' answered Mimir grimly. And from that day Odin had but one eye.

Mimir became Odin's counsellor, and very soon warned him that he must form an alliance with the Vanir, for the Æsir needed every ally they could find.

The Vanir were the shining ones who had been born out of the upper air and dwelt first in Uhland, above the high top of Yggdrasill. They never came to Asgard nor Midgard, nor ever even set foot upon firm ground: it seemed that they did not know of the Æsir's existence, nor did the Æsir know of them.

Odin sent forth his messengers to seek the Vanir in Uhland, but they sought in vain. So they cried aloud into the wide air that Odin and the Æsir would form a league with the Vanir, if the Vanir would but send one of their number to Asgard to speak with Odin.

No answer came. But one day a Giant maiden named Gullveig arrived in Asgard. She was only a little taller than the Æsir, and she was very fair to look upon: not only her hair and her eyes, but all her body seemed to shine like gold.

The Æsir welcomed her to their happy dwelling-place and she moved amongst them like a sunbeam while they sat under the leafy shade of Yggdrasill in the courtyards of their palaces playing at chess with golden chessmen, and at draughts with discs of gold.

But presently as Gullveig passed from one to another, and wandered down into Midgard, there seemed to come a shadow over the world. Odin noticed that mankind were no longer as happy and as open as they had been. Suddenly the love of gold had been born amongst them: they were making it into ring-money, hiding it away in secret places, plotting, cheating, murdering for the sake of what had before been merely the most useful and beautiful metal for making cups and ornaments.

Seeing this, Odin summoned the Æsir to meet in Valhalla, and set Gullveig in the middle of the floor before them.

'See!' he cried, 'the Giant maiden who has come among us! She is a witch and a sorceress, and has let loose Sin in Midgard where it was never known before! Now the Golden Age has ended – and our foes in Jotunheim have won another victory. Æsir of Asgard, my brothers and my sons, what doom for Gullveig, the mother of Sin?'

'The doom of death!' they cried with one voice, and rising all together they cast their spears at her. Through her body the keen weapons passed from every side and clattered on the golden floor. But Gullveig stood before them still, unharmed and laughing.

Then a great fire was built in the hall and Gullveig was placed on it and consumed to ashes. But when the flames died down, she stepped forth living and unharmed – shining and glittering more brightly than before.

Three times they burned her to ashes in the Hall of Odin, and thrice she stepped forth out of the fire, even fairer than before – even as gold that is smelted in the furnace grows richer and deeper and more valuable each time it is poured into the mould.

Then Gullveig stepped to the nearest door of Valhalla, and turning, cried to the Æsir: 'I have brought division among men, and you have brought division among gods! Behold now, I came as the messenger of the Vanir – and see how you have treated me! Now I return to tell them that there is no faith in Asgard: that there a guest is riddled with spears, the herald is cast on the fire. But my purpose is accomplished – and now there shall be war between the Æsir and the Vanir!'

So saying Gullveig sprang upon the nearest sunbeam and was gone out of Asgard in a moment.

Then the Æsir took council together, for Odin suspected that as Gullveig had cheated them, she was probably deceiving the Vanir as well and trying to bring about a war between them, which would give the Giants their chance of conquering Asgard.

Sure enough, before they had decided what to do, a great army of the Vanir came out of the clear sky and began tearing down the walls of Asgard.

Odin advanced against them and hurled his spear at the leader. But he caught it as it flew and returned it with a low bow.

'King of the Vanir, how are you named?' asked Odin.

'I am Niord, lord of Vanaheim,' replied the shining warrior, 'and I do not come against you in anger, but in sorrow for your treatment of my messenger.'

'If you speak of Gullveig the witch,' said Odin, 'she can be no messenger between Æsir and Vanir. For she is of the Jotun race, and her one desire is to bring ruin upon your people and upon mine – yes, and upon the dwellers in Midgard as well, so that the Giants may rule.'

He went on to tell how Sin had been let loose among men, and when Niord heard, and understood how desperate was the struggle which the Æsir waged against the Giants, he flung down his shining sword and clasped Odin by the hand.

'Let there be peace between us,' he cried, 'peace between Æsir and Vanir, between earth and air. We will help you against the Giants; we will be as one people; we will swear eternal friendship and exchange hostages.'

The Æsir rejoiced greatly at this, and Honir, Odin's brother, volunteered to go and live among the Vanir as a pledge of good faith.

'And I myself will remain here in Asgard,' said Niord.

'Be welcome then,' cried Odin, 'welcome not as a hostage of a different race, but as one of ourselves. Here you may build your palace and live as freely, and in as great honour as the Æsir live. In all our councils you shall have a place as if you were indeed my brother.'

So the union between the Vanir and the Æsir was sealed, and a solemn ceremony was held at which every one of the Æsir and Vanir swore an oath of loyalty to each other, and in token of good faith spat into a crock of gold.

Thus Niord came to live in Asgard, and there in after years were born his son Frey who became lord of the weather and master of agriculture, and his daughter Freya the lady of love and beauty, and splendid palaces were built for each of them.

Now Odin saw a way to gain still greater wisdom. He took the golden crock which was the seal of union between the Æsir and the Vanir, and by the arts which the wisdom of Mimir had already taught him, he made of it a man called Kvasir. This man came into being fully grown, remembering no childhood: but instead he was filled with all the knowledge both of the Vanir and the Æsir.

In Asgard he was loved for his goodness; but in

Midgard he was adored by all men for bringing peace among them, teaching them manners and showing them many of the arts and crafts which made their lives better and happier. Anyone who was in trouble, or in need of advice, had only to send for Kvasir, and he would go wherever he was needed.

But in the end this proved his undoing, for two wicked Dwarfs named Fialar and Galar begged him to come and advise them on a very private matter.

Kvasir in the goodness of his own heart could suspect no evil, so he went secretly to the Dwarfs and they, as soon as they had him deep in their hidden caves, murdered him and drew off his magic blood into two vats and a kettle.

Then they mixed honey with the blood of Kvasir and brewed with it a magic mead which had the power of making anyone who drank of it into a poet, a scholar, and a seer.

The Dwarfs made no use of this treasure, but merely gloated over it in secret. To account for his disappearance they put it about that Kvasir had been worn out by his own cleverness, and had choked for lack of anyone who could carry on an argument with him.

No one seemed to suspect them, so the wicked couple decided to murder a Giant as well. First they invited a certain Gilling and his wife to visit them and entertained them very kindly.

On the first morning they suggested that Gilling

should come out in their boat with them while they caught fish for breakfast.

'Then you must row carefully,' said the Giant, 'for I cannot swim.'

Fialar winked at Galar, and away they went over the smooth sea. But on the return journey they steered the boat into rough water by some overhanging rocks, and it was upset. Gilling was drowned, but the Dwarfs who were excellent swimmers righted the boat and rowed home again.

When they told the Giant's wife that Gilling had fallen out of the boat and tipped it up trying to climb in again, she shrieked and wept until they were nearly deafened.

'Come with me!' shouted Fialar at last. 'I'll take you to a door of our caves from which you can see the very place where your husband was drowned. Surely that will comfort you!'

The Giantess agreed to this, and while she was getting ready to follow him, Fialar drew his brother aside and said in a low voice:

'Now's our chance to kill her too! Go to the window above.'

Having given Galar a little time, Fialar led the Giantess through the caves to a doorway looking towards the sea.

'Walk out through there,' he told her, 'and you will be so near where your husband was drowned that you'll almost find yourself with him.'

Suspecting nothing, she went forward quickly through the doorway, and Galra dropped a millstone on her head from the window above and killed her.

Gilling's son, Suttung, was, however, suspicious about the mysterious disappearance of both his parents, and he arrived at the Dwarfs' cave before they could hide the body of the Giantess.

Fialar and Galar were so terrified when the great Giant Suttung suddenly pounced on them, that they made no attempt to deny what they had done.

'So,' rumbled the Giant. 'You killed my parents with water and with rock, and they both died quickly. Now I'm going to kill you in the same way – with water and with rock – but as slowly as I can.'

Then he carried them far out to sea and set them down on a low ridge of rock.

'The tide is out now as far as it goes,' he told them. 'At this time of year the rock you are on is never quite covered even when the tide is high. But in a few weeks' time high tide will cover the rock and sweep you off into the sea. Even Dwarfs can't swim to land from here but I know you can live without food for several months . . . so you'll have plenty of time to think what it's like to be drowned, and I'll come every day to see how you are getting on!'

Giant Suttung went away over the sea, laughing grimly to himself, and the two Dwarfs huddled miserably on the rock as the cold northern night gathered about them.

Several days went by, and they grew more and more wretched and frightened as the tide came higher and higher, until at last, even on the highest point of the rock, the sea came up to their knees.

Each day Giant Suttung came to gloat over them, and shouted jeering remarks in answer to their prayers for mercy.

'We'll pay you a huge ransom!' they cried. 'Mountains of gold and treasure. We'll work for you and make cunning tools and weapons!'

'I've all the gold I want,' answered Suttung, 'and what use are tools to me? All I want is plenty to eat and drink, and to spend my life comfortably without doing any work.'

Then the Dwarfs remembered the magic mead which they had made from the blood of Kvasir, and Fialar cried:

'Noble Giant, we will give you the most precious thing in the world, a drink which even the Æsir do not possess – a drink for which great Odin himself would give his other eye!'

'What drink is that?' growled the Giant.

'It is called the Mead of Inspiration,' answered the Dwarfs, 'or so we have heard – for we do not know what Inspiration means. But we have tasted it, and no mead in the world is so good. It was made from the blood of Kvasir the Wise, which we mingled with honey – and it makes one more deliciously drunk than any other mead. But when you're drunk, instead of falling under the table, you get up and talk and sing: and nobody can resist what you say. That's how we got the better of your mother and father.'

Thinking that there might be something to this, and also being anxious to prevent the Æsir from ever possessing the precious drink, Suttung at last took the two shivering Dwarfs to land.

In return they handed over the three vessels containing the precious liquor, and Suttung took it away to his castle on a mountain on the borders of Jotunheim. There he stored it away in his treasure chamber which was hollowed out of the solid rock in the very heart of the mountain.

Now Odin knew nothing of what had happened. For the wise Mimir had left him and gone with Honir to live in Vanaheim, the chief dwelling-place of the Vanir. There a quarrel broke out between Mimir and the lords of the Vanir, for it seemed to them that he had cast a spell upon Honir who on a sudden could not answer any question they put to him, but would always reply: 'Mimir must answer that.'

At last, thinking that Mimir must be a sorcerer or warlock, they killed him and sent his head to the Æsir.

Odin grieved greatly over Mimir's death, but he did not seek to be revenged on the Vanir, feeling sure that they must have acted under some misunderstanding.

But by his arts he kept the head of Mimir from decay, and set it beside the Fountain of Wisdom which had been Mimir's well, and from that day the head of Mimir kept him warned of dangers to come, telling him what should be avoided.

The very first thing the magic head told him was about Kvasir's death and the Mead of Inspiration.

'You must win that mead and bear it to Asgard,' the head told him. 'Not a drop should be left with the Giants. Suttung has it now in his castle, but he has not yet dared to taste it.'

When Odin had learnt the whole story of Suttung's revenge, he called a council in Asgard and told the other Æsir all that had happened.

'We cannot send to demand or buy the mead,' he said, 'for that would show the Giant how anxious we are to have it. Someone must go in disguise and try to win or steal it.'

No one seemed anxious to attempt this desperate venture, and it was Odin himself who set out next day, disguised as an old farm labourer.

With a broad-brimmed hat pulled down over his blind eye, and a scythe on his shoulder, Odin strode through Midgard, until he came to the lands on the edge of Jotunheim where Baugi, Suttung's brother, lived.

Out in the fields he found nine men mowing a meadow of hay, and he stopped to talk with them.

'How do you enjoy working for a Giant?' he asked.

'Well enough,' answered one of the mowers, 'but we cannot keep our scythes sharp enough to mow as quickly as Master Baugi wants.'

'That is easily remedied,' said the disguised Odin, 'let me sharpen them for you.'

He took his hone out of his belt, and set to work. When he had finished, the scythes cut like razors and the men were amazed.

'I should like to buy that hone!' cried one of them. 'Stranger, will you sell?'

'No, no!' exclaimed another, pushing in front of him. 'Sell it to me! I have more money, since Master Baugi gave me richer reward after we followed him beyond Mirk Wood to sack and burn the houses there.'

So each tried harder and harder to outbid the others, and in their excitement told Odin far more about their own wicked deeds than they intended; and at last he cried:

'I'll sell the hone for a thousand rings of money. Now, he who catches it shall have it!'

With that he tossed it into the air suddenly, and each of the nine men sprang forward to catch it as it fell. But they all met in a confused mass, still holding their razor-like scythes; and every man of them got his death from the sharp blades.

When Odin saw that a just doom had befallen them, he picked up his hone, flung his cloak about him, and went on his way.

That night he came to the house of Baugi the Giant, and asked for shelter.

'I am a poor labouring man,' he said, 'and my name is Bolverker. I am not unskilled in the evil arts, as my name shows – and I can earn my night's lodging.'

'Bolverker or Bale Worker, it's all the same to me,' grumbled Baugi. 'One man is no use, however skilled in evil. How am I going to get my harvest in? Those nine men of mine seem to have had a fight amongst themselves and killed one another. I wouldn't have minded so much if they had cut the hay first. But where I'm to get more men from now I don't know. I've killed most of the people round here, and chased the rest away. These nine were my special followers: mowers of hay in the summer, and mowers of men in the winter! . . . One man is no good.'

'You should try me before you taunt me,' remarked Odin, leaning on his scythe. 'What will you give me if I do your nine men's work in less time than they would have taken?'

'Give you?' repeated the Giant, staring stupidly at Odin. 'It is not possible. But *if* you can do it, I'll give you anything you ask for.'

'Well,' said Odin, 'I've heard that your brother, the great Giant Suttung, has a very fine mead in his cellars called Kvasir's Blood. Give me one drink of that, and I'll harvest your crops better than you've ever had them harvested before.'

'Kvasir's Blood!' rumbled Baugi, rubbing his nose. 'Suttung will never give you even a sip of that! Why, he won't even give me any.'

'Well, will you promise to help me get a drink of it without him knowing?' suggested Odin. 'A

Giant like you and a Bale Worker like me ought to be able to find a way.'

'Oh, I'll promise that,' said Baugi. 'But you'll have to be as cunning as a whole mountain of Dwarfs to do it.'

Once the oath was sworn, Odin in his disguise set to work. He had the haycrop scythed and carted and made into neat little stacks before the corn was ripe. Then he reaped the cornfields too, dried and threshed the grain and stored it away in Baugi's granaries.

'Well, master Bolverker,' said the Giant when he had seen that all was done. 'You've worked harder than nine men, and you've earned a better reward than even a drink of brother Suttung's precious mead. Come with me to his castle and I'll see if I can persuade him to reward you as you deserve.'

So Odin went with Baugi to the castle of Suttung, but when the Giant heard his brother's request, he refused flatly. Indeed he flew into a great rage.

'You were always a fool, Baugi,' he roared. 'I have secret information that our enemies the Æsir themselves want my mead – and you'd waste it on a good-for-nothing farmhand, just because he cuts hay better than those robbers of yours. This mead of mine must be precious indeed if Odin himself desires it. So I'm not even going to drink it myself just yet. It's down in my treasure vault under the mountain where no one can get at it.

And, just to make quite sure, my daughter
Gunnlod is locked up with it as its guardian. I put
her there as soon as I heard that the Æsir wanted
it. Now go back to your farm, and if you don't
take this Bolverker with you, I'll make *his* blood
into mead. And I won't waste time drinking that,
I can tell you!'

Off went Baugi, looking very angry and rather
foolish, and Odin walked behind him, thinking
hard.

'I fear there's no way of getting you your drink,
friend Bolverker,' said Baugi at last. 'When my
brother makes up his mind, no one can persuade
him to change it.'

'Remember the rest of your promise,' said Odin.
'If Suttung would not give me a cup of the mead,
you were to help me to take one without his knowledge.'

'Oh, I'll help you if you can find a way,' grunted
Baugi. 'But you heard what he said? Under the
mountain, and guarded by Gunnlod.'

'We'll manage it all the same,' answered Odin.
'Just take me to the nearest place to this cave
where Suttung keeps it.'

Looking puzzled, Baugi led him into a cave
under the mountain, and at last paused in front of
a solid wall of rock.

'This is the nearest place outside the castle
itself,' he said. 'But there's half a mountain of
solid rock between here and Suttung's cellar.'

'If you do as I tell you, I'll get all I want,'

answered Odin. With that he took an auger out of his pocket and handed it to Baugi.

'This is a magic auger,' he said. 'As you bore with it, it gets longer and longer no matter how deep you drill; and it only stops when it comes out the other side. The rock's too hard for me, but a Giant like you ought to be able to use it.'

More puzzled than ever, Baugi took the auger in both hands and set to work boring a hole straight into the stone. On and on he worked, until he began to grow tired. At last he pulled out the auger and flung it down exclaiming:

'There! I'm right through! But what the use of that little hole is, I don't know!'

Odin bent down and blew into the hole, and as he did so the chips of stone flew out into his face.

'Giant Baugi,' he said reproachfully, 'I did not think you would cheat me after all I have done for you.'

With an angry grunt Baugi picked up the auger and set to work again. This time he went on until it went through the rock to the other side.

Odin blew into the hole again, and as the dust did not fly back, he knew that the hole went right through.

'Now stay here on guard,' he said, and he turned himself into a snake, and wriggled into the hole.

Even Baugi realized now that Bolverker was something more than an ordinary farm labourer who had dabbled in black magic.

'This must be a thief from the Æsir,' he thought. 'He may even be one of the Æsir!'

So thinking he snatched up the auger and thrust it into the hole, meaning to kill the snake.

Odin, however, suspected treachery, and changed himself into a worm as soon as he was inside the hole, so that he was able to avoid the auger.

Then he crawled out into Suttung's treasure chamber, and changed himself from a worm into a handsome young Giant.

Gunnlod, Suttung's beautiful daughter, was very surprised to see him.

'I suppose you have come here by magic for a drink of the mead made of Kvasir's Blood,' she said. 'I am here to guard it. But I'm so tired of being shut up in this dark cave, that I won't tell my father about you. If you'll kiss me, I will let you drink the mead out of one of the vats in which it is stored.'

Odin gave her a kiss and she was so pleased that she opened the first of the vats and told him to help himself.

Then Odin called all his knowledge of sorcery into play. He lifted the great vat to his lips and emptied it at a draught.

'A great thirst you have, stranger prince,' said Gunnlod looking at him wide-eyed with wonder.

'Ah,' replied Odin craftily, 'but my thirst for the mead is nothing compared with my thirst for another kiss from the divine lips of the lovely lady Gunnlod!'

Like all Giants Gunnlod was very slow-witted, and now she was so thrilled at being admired by this handsome young Giant who could empty a whole vat of mead at one draught, that she put up her lips for another kiss. When she had received it, Odin took the second vat.

'To Gunnlod, loveliest of the Giant kind!' he cried, and drained it to the dregs.

Gunnlod was completely captivated, and desired nothing in the world so much as the love of this wonderful young Giant.

'Kiss me again!' she begged. 'Kiss me, and you may drink from the golden Kettle which holds the richest draught of Kvasir's Blood.'

Odin needed no second bidding. But when he had drained the kettle as well, he lay back utterly exhausted.

'Wonderful Giant,' cried Gunnlod, 'I cannot live without you. Be my husband, and whatever I can give you shall be yours.'

'First give me air, and a sight of the blue sky!' gasped Odin.

Then Gunnlod, suspecting nothing, opened a door at the top of a great shaft in the rock which led down to the deep Treasure Chamber where they were.

At once Odin turned himself into an eagle, and flew triumphantly out into the open air.

Now Gunnlod realized how she had been tricked, and her shrieks quickly brought Suttung to her side.

As soon as he learnt what had happened, he turned himself into an eagle also, and flew off in pursuit of Odin.

Meanwhile the Æsir were waiting on the walls of Asgard, straining anxious eyes towards the north.

When at last they saw a great eagle flying out of the darkness towards them, they knew it was Odin, and made ready to receive him as he had instructed them before he set out on his dangerous expedition. They placed three golden vessels ready in the courtyard, and then took their stand on the wall once more, with drawn swords in their hands, while Uller fitted an arrow to his bow.

Nearer and nearer came the eagle, shining in the darkness; and now the Æsir could see another eagle which pursued him and was gaining on him fast – a great black eagle, with mighty wings almost as big as those of Raesvelg, the Giant who made the tempests.

Over the wall came the shining eagle, and the moment he touched the golden pavement of Asgard there was a flash of light, and Odin stood there; and in the same instant the three golden vessels were filled to the brim with the Mead of Inspiration.

But even as the Giant Suttung reached the wall, and as Uller drew his bow to shoot, the sun rose above the eastern mountains. Its first beam fell on Suttung, and at once the eagle cloak dropped from him, and he crashed to the ground, a great lump of stone.

'So shall it be with all the Giant kind,' said Odin solemnly. 'If the sun shines upon them in the holy land of Asgard, the evil that is in them shall weigh them down, and they will turn into stone.

'But now we have Kvasir's Blood among us, and in time it shall be given to those men of Midgard whom we think fit. They shall be poets; they shall sing of the deeds of gods and heroes, and tell mighty sagas of the doings of men and women whom the Norns lead to do brave deeds or suffer grievous sorrows bravely.

'Come now, let us drink of the Mead of Inspiration, so that our own wisdom may be increased; for we shall need all our skill to keep the Giants out of Asgard. This my theft of Kvasir's Blood and the deceit which I was obliged to practise on the Giantess Gunnlod have, alas, brought sin into Asgard that cannot be banished as easily as Gullveig – who shall enter no more now that the Vanir are with us.

'Who shall be the Betrayer even wise Mimir has not yet made known to me. But I fear that it will be one of our own number – for so the Runes of Knowledge seem to tell me – those magic writings which now I can read since I have drunk the Blood of Kvasir.'

Then for a while there was silence in Asgard as Odin strove in vain to see into the future. But even the blood of Kvasir could not give him this power.

3

THE APPLES OF IDUNA

In the early days of the world there came a boat
sailing over the sea in the fair summer weather. In
it sat a handsome youth who played upon a golden
harp and sang sweetly to the white gulls who flew
around him. Presently the boat touched the shore
as near to Asgard as the bright sea came, and the
minstrel stepped on to the land.

As he went forward green grass sprang up out
of the bare earth all round him, and after the grass
came flowers. Then the birds sang, and the small
animals frisked and frolicked on either side.

As he drew nearer to Asgard the Æsir heard the

sweet strains of his harp and hastened across the Bridge Bifrost to meet him.

But before they came, the earth shook and opened beside him, and out stepped a lovely maiden, as fair as the spring itself, carrying in her hands a casket of gold.

The minstrel seemed to expect her, for he held out his hand, and she took it in hers, so that when they came to the foot of Bifrost they were walking hand in hand.

'Welcome to you, great lords of Asgard!' cried the minstrel. 'I come to you out of Jotunheim where the Giants dwell, yet I am one of your-selves. Gunnlod the beautiful is my mother, she who guarded the Mead of Inspiration made from the blood of Kvasir. Odin is my father, for he wedded her in the treasure vault of Suttung. The blood of Kvasir flows in my veins, and I am here to sing and play for you in Asgard.'

'Welcome to you, my son Bragi, Lord of Poesy and sweet Music,' said Odin. 'My wisdom told me that you would come, and with you great joy to the Æsir.'

'I bring you joy indeed,' answered Bragi, and he led forward the lovely Earth-maiden who walked beside him. 'This is my bride to be, Iduna the Beautiful, the daughter of Ivaldi the Earth Dwarf.'

'Welcome to Asgard, Iduna, Lady of Youth,' said Odin. 'Now tell us, I pray, what you carry with you in your casket of gold?'

'I bring you the Apples of Youth,' answered Iduna in a voice as soft and sweet as water tinkling into a mountain pool. 'Of these you shall eat and be young and strong for ever.'

'Welcome, thrice welcome to Asgard!' cried Odin, his face shining with joy. 'Even the gods grow old, and we have need of youth and strength if we are to fight against the Giants and bring fair gifts to the dwellers in Midgard.

'Now come both of you into Asgard, and tonight we shall hold your wedding feast with rejoicing such as we have never known before.'

So the wedding of Bragi and Iduna took place that night, and ever afterwards they dwelt among the Æsir. And at the ending of a feast Iduna would glide softly about the banquet hall and give to each of them an apple from her golden casket, and they would eat and feel youth course through their veins more strongly than ever. And however many apples were given by Iduna to the Æsir, her casket remained always full.

Of course the Giants, when they heard of this wonder, were anxious to steal the apples for themselves. But for a long time they strove in vain: for none of them could creep into Asgard, and Iduna never took her apples down into the plains of Midgard.

One day, however, Odin and his brother, Honir the shining one, set out through Midgard disguised as ordinary travellers, observing the joys and sorrows, the labours and pastimes of mortal men.

They went fast and far, and on their journey they came to the mountains not far from the borders of Jotunheim.

As they wandered through the valleys and pine forests, a young man met them, fair to look upon, with twinkling, mischievous eyes.

'Greetings to you, Odin and Honir, mighty Æsir, sons of Borr and Bestla!' he cried.

Odin frowned, and answered severely:

'Young sir, how comes it that you are so familiar with our names and state? Surely some magic of the Giants is in this?'

'No magic at all,' answered the stranger. 'For I am your cousin, and my name is Loki. True, the Giant blood is in my veins, but it runs in yours also, I believe. For Bestla's father was Bælthorn the Giant, and his brother Bergelmir was father to my father Farbauti . . . So I beg you, my cousins, let me join you on your wanderings and prove if I am worthy to stand with the Æsir in their struggle against the evil Giants who dwell in Jotunheim.'

So Loki went with Odin and Honir, and helped them in their work. And he soon proved that he would be useful to the guardians of Asgard, for his cleverness and cunning were very great; he was always ready with some plan to help them out of a difficulty. Also he had, like Odin, the power of changing himself into any shape he wished.

One day, however, he met with a power greater than his own, and showed that he was by no means free from the evil of the Giant race.

With Odin and Honir, he had been wandering over mountains and waste places, where food was hard to find. But when they came down into a certain lonely valley they saw a herd of oxen grazing there.

One of these oxen they took and killed, and clever Loki kindled a fire by means of two sticks rubbed together, and set about cooking them a huge dinner.

After a time Loki thought that the meat must be cooked, so he took the spit from the fire and was about to carve the great piece of meat when, to his amazement, he saw that it was still completely raw.

He set it back over the fiercest part of the fire, and left it there for half an hour more.

At the end of that time Honir exclaimed:

'Surely the ox must be cooked by now! Where is your usual skill, Loki?'

Then Loki told them what had happened: 'And I think there is something strange about this,' he ended, 'so will both of you examine the fire before I take off the meat – and the meat as soon as it is clear of the fire?'

Loki scattered the fire and lifted off the beef.

'Look!' he exclaimed. 'It's as raw as when we had just flayed the beast! Yet it has been over the fire for nearly two hours!'

The two Æsir examined it, and saw to their surprise that Loki was quite correct.

'There must be evil magic at work here,' said Odin.

'Ha! ha!' cried a harsh voice in the great tree above them. 'You will never cook that meat without my help!'

They looked up in surprise, and there sat a great eagle.

'Will you help us, then?' said Loki, who was the first to recover from his surprise.

'Yes, I'll help you!' cried the eagle. 'But you must promise that when the ox is cooked you will let me eat as much as I want before you start.'

The Æsir agreed, for they were very hungry, and the eagle flew down and fanned the fire into a blaze with his big wings.

When Loki pushed away the burning branches and took the ox from its skewer, it was beautifully cooked right through.

'Now I'll take my portion,' said the eagle, 'and then you can begin your meal!'

So saying, he helped himself to all four legs, hams, loins and shoulders.

'Stop!' shouted Loki, springing up in a rage. 'You've taken far more than your share, and not left enough for the three of us. Why, I myself could easily eat all that remains!'

The eagle paid no attention, but sat back gorging the roast beef and chuckling to itself.

Then Loki lost his temper completely. He picked up a branch which lay near by and struck the eagle with it, shouting:

'Give us back some of the meat, you greedy brute!'

At once the eagle rose into the air and flew away. But the branch had stuck to his feathers, and Loki was stuck to the branch. Struggle as hard as he could, neither would come loose.

Down swooped the eagle as soon as they drew near to a mountain-side, and Loki was dragged over sharp stones and rocks, through trees and thorn bushes and brambles, till he was in a sorry state. He felt as though his arms would be torn from their sockets at any moment.

So he began to beg for his life, and offer the eagle any reward he chose to name.

'Bring Iduna out of Asgard, with her casket of apples, and I will take you back to your friends and restore your dinner,' answered the eagle.

Loki refused indignantly. 'I could not do that even if I wanted to,' he ended. 'I am not yet one of the Æsir, and I doubt if they would even let me into Asgard.'

'Then I'll drag you from end to end of Midgard and back again,' screamed the eagle fiercely. 'Know that I am Thiassi the Storm Giant – and what I have done is nothing to what I am able to do!'

Loki was very frightened when he heard this, and he at once promised to do everything in his power to bring Iduna and her apples out of Asgard.

So Thiassi carried him back to where Odin and Honir were still waiting by the fire, released him from the branch, and returned both hind legs of the ox to the hungry Æsir.

Loki did not tell Odin and Honir of the bargain he had made, nor even that the eagle was in reality a Storm Giant. He said only that he had been justly punished for striking the eagle – to whom, he added, the ox they had killed really belonged – and that it had forgiven him and returned some of the meat to make up for the punishment it had given him.

Odin suspected nothing, and indeed seemed so pleased with Loki that when they returned to Asgard he gave him a dwelling-place in Midgard near the foot of Bifrost Bridge, and often went down there to consult him.

Loki worked hard and well for the Æsir. But he did not forget his promise to Thiassi the Storm Giant, and his crafty mind was busy with schemes for luring Iduna out of Asgard by herself – with her magic apples.

One day she and Bragi came to walk in the pleasant meadows and woods of Midgard, and when she became separated from Bragi for a few moments Loki met her in disguise and said:

'Lady Iduna, I have heard much of the wonderful apples you keep in Asgard. Not far from here is a little wood where grow just such apples as yours, only these I am sure both look and taste far fairer than yours.'

'I cannot believe that,' answered Iduna. 'But if it could be true, then it is my duty to pluck these apples of which you speak. For only the Æsir must eat of them.'

'If only you had your own apples with you,' said Loki, 'you could compare them with the apples which I have found.'

'I have not brought them,' answered Iduna, suspecting no evil. 'But I shall come back tomorrow, and bring my casket with me from Asgard. I cannot rest until I know what apples these are which you have found ... For I believed that kind Mother Earth had yielded only the one crop of the Apples of Youth – that crop which she entrusted to me.'

When Iduna had gone back to find Bragi, Loki made haste to inform the Giant Thiassi of the chance which he would have on the morrow.

And next day he was waiting in the same disguise near the foot of Bifrost from the moment when the bright Sun chariot set out across the sky.

Early in the afternoon Iduna came down the shining rainbow bridge, as young and lovely as the spring itself, and carrying the golden casket in her hands.

Loki lost no time in taking her out of sight under the trees, and as soon as they were well away from Asgard, he begged her to wait a moment, then slipped quickly back by the path they had come. As soon as he reached the edge of the wood, he cast off his disguise, and for the rest of the day walked in the plain below Asgard hoping that Odin or one of the Æsir might see him.

Meanwhile the great eagle had swooped down

upon Iduna and carried her away – away over Midgard and deep into Jotunheim, until he came to Thrymheim, the Kingdom of the Winds.

There he set her down in a mighty castle built on the top of a bare rocky mountain round which the tempests raged and wailed day and night without ceasing.

Then he cast off his eagle disguise and stood before poor, trembling Iduna in his own terrible Giant form.

'I am Thiassi the Storm Giant!' he cried. 'And this is my stronghold, far from Asgard, far from any help that the Æsir could render you. Here you must stay, and if you will give me to eat of your magic Apples of Youth, I will make you my wife and Queen of Thrymheim.'

'Never, never!' cried Iduna bravely. 'These apples are for the Æsir alone, and no Giant lips shall ever touch them. Nor can I ever be your queen, for I am the wife of Bragi the divine minstrel, master of all sweet songs.'

At that Thiassi roared with rage until the very castle shook beneath his hurricane breath.

'Here you shall stay!' he shrieked. 'Here, alone, until you grant what I wish!' So saying he shut Iduna into the highest room of the tower above the castle, and went raging away, spreading havoc through Jotunheim, and over Midgard.

Meanwhile in Asgard the Æsir began to miss the nightly visits of Iduna to the banqueting hall with her golden casket of magic fruit.

'Where is Iduna?' they asked, and Bragi could only shake his head sadly and strike a melancholy tune from the strings of his golden harp.

'She has gone from me, and I know not whither,' he sighed. 'Out of the earth she came to me: perhaps she has returned into the earth . . . But surely she will come again.'

Age now began to touch the Æsir. There came a streak of silver even into Baldur's golden hair; Odin's limbs grew stiff, and Thor himself felt the weight of years upon his mighty shoulders.

Odin could learn nothing of Iduna: even from Lidskialf he could not see what had become of her, nor would Mimir's Head prophesy of her return.

But Hugin and Munin, Odin's ravens, flew fast and far: over all Midgard and day by day deeper into Jotunheim. And at last they brought back news:

'Iduna is in the tall tower above the castle of Thiassi the Storm Giant in windy Thrymheim,' they croaked. 'She keeps the Apples of Youth safely in their golden casket, and Thiassi cannot touch them. But she grows pale and wan as she sits in the high window gazing, gazing towards Asgard and calling in vain upon Bragi to come to her aid.'

Then Odin gathered the Æsir in council, and told them what he had learned.

'We must attack Jotunheim and kill every Giant in it!' shouted Thor in his voice of thunder. 'There is not a moment to be lost, for we grow old already!'

Odin smiled and shook his head.

'You were ever in a hurry, my son,' he said. 'You have always believed that strength will accomplish everything, and patience nothing. Even as a babe your kindly mother Jord could not control you – and I well remember how you first showed your mighty strength by lifting ten loads of bearskins which she had piled upon you in a vain effort to keep you in your cradle. No, this time cunning is our only chance . . . But I do not know who can help us, for the Giants are on guard, and I cannot slip into Jotunheim in disguise as easily as I did when I won the Mead of Inspiration out of Suttung's treasure vault.'

Then Honir the shining one spoke, for he was in Asgard on a visit from the Vanir with whom his home now was.

'I remember when last we went through the world,' he said, 'that a certain Loki, who seemed half a Giant, and yet more like one of us Æsir, came with us. And whatever trouble we met, he got us out of it easily by his cunning.'

'Well remembered, my brother,' cried Odin. 'Loki is the person we want. He lives now in Midgard, not far from the foot of Bifrost, and I visit him from time to time to seek advice from him.'

So Odin and many of the Æsir went down over Bifrost Bridge and found Loki in his wood nearby.

When they told him about the theft of Iduna and her apples, and asked him if he could help to get her back, Loki looked very grave.

'I might be able to rescue the Lady Iduna,' he said at length, 'but it will be hard and dangerous . . . My greatest difficulty is that I am not one of the Æsir and, being of the Giant kin myself, I cannot enter Asgard.'

'If you can bring back Iduna safely, and with her the Apples of Youth, we will make you one of ourselves,' said Odin. 'But you must also swear to be loyal and faithful in our war against the Giants.'

Loki agreed to this, binding himself by terrible oaths which would bring upon him the most dreadful punishments if he broke them. Then Odin solemnly made him his blood-brother, and said:

'Now the blood of the Æsir flows in your veins, and you may enter Asgard as one of ourselves. Nevertheless, swift and terrible shall be your doom if you enter it and do not bring back Iduna the beautiful and her magic apples.'

'I go to fetch her from Thrymheim,' answered Loki triumphantly. 'Meanwhile make ready a great fire of shavings and resinous pine in the very gateway of Asgard. But do not kindle it until the moment arrives . . . Remember that I can change into any shape I wish, but Thiassi the Storm Giant can take only the form of a monstrous eagle.'

Loki set out, walking swiftly. But as soon as he

was out of sight of the Æsir he turned himself into a falcon and flew off in the direction of Thrymheim. When he reached the castle, he flew round it for some time, listening to what the Giant warriors and servants were saying. From their conversation he learnt that Thiassi had gone out fishing, and that Iduna was quite alone up in her prison in the tower.

So he flew boldly in through the window, and found Iduna sitting sadly there with her beautiful face resting on her hands, gazing, ever gazing out towards the bright spring lands beyond wintery Jotunheim.

'Lady Iduna!' he cried. 'Quickly! I have come from Asgard to rescue you – to carry you back to your husband! Take the golden casket with the Apples of Youth in it, hold it firmly whatever happens, and trust to me.'

Iduna sprang up eagerly, wrapped her cloak about her, snatched up the golden casket, and, clasping it firmly to her breast, she exclaimed:

'O blessed bird out of the world of light and summer, I am ready! Only take me in safety to Asgard, and the falcon shall be for ever the friend of the Æsir and of the dwellers in Midgard – the bird whom no man would hurt.'

Then Loki the falcon turned Iduna into the shape and size of a nut, seized her in his claws, and flew swiftly out of the window.

In a little while the Giant Thiassi returned home, and went up to the room in the tower-top.

When he found that both Iduna and her apples were gone, his rage was so violent that the very tower came tumbling down into the courtyard.

'No one has been here!' cried the trembling servants. 'And no creature either, save for a falcon which hovered about for some time. Then it flew in through the tower window, and a few moments later flew out again carrying what looked like a sparrow – for on such small birds these hawks delight to feed. It flew away not long ago, over the mountains towards Midgard.'

Then Thiassi took upon himself the shape of a mighty eagle, so great that his wings seemed to stretch across the sky. He leapt into the air, and the winds went shrieking after him as he soared up and away. With a mighty rushing sound he tore across Jotunheim and over Midgard; and beneath his flight the trees were wrenched from the ground and the yellow corn was beaten flat; great castles fell, houses and haystacks were scattered and ships at sea were tossed upon the rocks or overwhelmed by the mountainous waves.

In Asgard the Æsir waited by the great gateway, looking anxiously out over Midgard towards Jotunheim.

Suddenly Heimdall the far-sighted cried:

'I see a falcon flying from Jotunheim, and it holds in its claws a nut! It is flying fast in this direction . . . Now, far behind it I see an eagle: never was there so great an eagle in Midgard. The eagle flies faster than the falcon and it is overtaking it!'

Now the Æsir themselves could see the valiant falcon with the nut in its claws flying towards them. And they saw the black eagle, growing bigger and bigger as it tore through the air behind it. They could see the forests bowing beneath the wings of the eagle and the corn lying flat as it passed over Midgard, and they knew that it was Thiassi the Storm Giant.

Watching eagerly, the Æsir took lighted torches and stood on either side of the great heap of shavings and resinous wood in the gate where Bifrost Bridge entered Asgard.

Nearer and nearer came the falcon, but it was almost spent, and nearer too drew the giant eagle. There were only a few yards of space between them when the falcon swooped through the gateway and down into the shadow of the wall.

Instantly the Æsir flung their torches into the heap, and the flames roared up suddenly as the eagle, unable to stop in his flight as he missed the falcon, plunged in through the gateway.

Straight into the flames went the eagle, and the feathers of his wings caught fire so that he fell in the gate of the Æsir, and died there beneath the sharp blades of swords, and spears, and battle-axes.

The Æsir turned from the dead Giant Thiassi, and saw Loki standing in the shadow of the wall. Beside him stood Iduna with the golden casket in her hands, and with a glad cry she ran forward and Bragi clasped her in his arms.

That night Loki took his place among the Æsir at the great feast, and ate with them of the Apples of Youth at the feast's ending. And ever afterwards they accepted him, even as they had accepted Niord, King of the Vanir, as one of themselves.

But although Thiassi was dead and Iduna with her apples was once more in Asgard, the danger from the Storm Giants was not yet over.

Next day there came striding across Midgard a Giant maiden dressed in glittering armour and waving a spear in her hand.

'I am Skadi, daughter of Thiassi the Storm Giant!' she cried. 'And I come to demand vengeance for the death of my father. If you do not grant it, I can take it easily, for Thiassi had two brothers, Idi and Gang, each as strong and as mighty as he was!'

Then Odin, standing in the gate of the Æsir, replied:

'Skadi, we do not wish to fight with you. So we offer you recompense for the death of your father. And we offer friendship to you and your kin. Say now how much gold the blood-price must be.'

Then Skadi cried out: 'We have more gold than there is in all Asgard. Do you not know that when the Giant Olvaldi died and his three sons, Thiassi, Idi and Gang, came to measure his gold, there was so much that no scales in the world would hold a tithe of it, so they had to divide it out in mouthfuls? No, you must give me a husband from among the Æsir, and you must make me laugh – a thing which I have never done.'

The Æsir discussed her offer among themselves, and it seemed to them wise to fall in with her wishes: for Skadi was very beautiful, and an alliance with the Storm Giants necessary, if Midgard and Asgard were not to be destroyed by them.

So Odin made answer: 'We agree to your terms, warrior maiden. But you must choose your husband by the feet only, seeing no more of him until after your choice is made.'

Skadi agreed to this, and Odin led her up into Asgard where she stood in her shining armour seeming little taller than anyone there. Then he led her on, into the great hall, and showed her a curtain behind which all the Æsir stood, with only their feet visible.

Skadi examined their feet, and when she came to one pair far more fair than any of the rest, she exclaimed:

'I choose this husband: I could not have a better mate than Baldur!'

But when the curtain was drawn aside, she saw that it was not Baldur but Niord of Vanaheim whom she had chosen.

Nevertheless both of them were content, and the wedding feast was held that night, and Loki played such merry antics with a goat that Skadi laughed aloud, and so the compact was sealed.

Trouble came between them very soon, however, for Niord wished to dwell in his castle of Noatun near the sea, while Skadi longed for her windy home in Thrymheim. They made an agreement then that they should dwell nine nights in Thrymheim, and the next nine in Noatun. But when Niord returned to his castle, he cried:

'Oh, how I loathed the hills! How horrible the wailing of the wolves sounded after the song of the birds!'

Skadi, however, said just the opposite: 'Here, I can never sleep on account of the wailing of the sea-birds. And if I do fall asleep, the sea-mew wakes me before the morning.'

So she spent more and more of her time up in the mountains, speeding about on her snowshoes, shooting bears with her swift arrows. But nevertheless in lovely Noatun by the sea two wondrous children were born to Skadi and Niord: a son called Frey and a daughter called Freya.

When they were grown they went to live in Asgard, and none were more loved and honoured among the Æsir than Frey, the Lord of Fruitfulness and bounteous Peace, and Freya, Lady of Love and Beauty – who nevertheless would go forth to battle at Odin's side driving her golden chariot drawn by two cats.

4

LOKI AND THE GIANTS

Loki now lived in Asgard, accepted as one of the
Æsir, and no one seemed to suspect that he had
first betrayed Iduna to the Storm Giant and then
won her back.

Indeed this was ever Loki's way, for he took
such a delight in mischief that he would often do
whatever came into his head, without counting
the cost. Nevertheless his cunning was very great,
and his powers were often useful to the Æsir.
Indeed at first he was one of the most important
guardians of Asgard, and saved them from disaster
more than once.

Odin believed that Loki had overcome and would forget his Giant nature; and remembering that he had made him his blood-brother, he saw to it that he was treated as if he were in truth Bestla's child and not merely her cousin's son.

Very early in the history of Midgard, Loki showed his prowess by dealing with the Giant Skrymsli who proved too much for both Odin and Honir.

For it chanced that the three Æsir were wandering the earth once more, as they did frequently in those early days, and came to the house of a farmer in the Faroe Islands.

The farmer, who did not recognize them in their disguise, welcomed the three travellers into his kitchen and set a good supper before them. But he did not make one of the party as they made merry round the fire with their horns of mead, and Odin noticed that he turned aside from time to time to weep.

'What troubles you, kind host?' asked Odin at length. 'Is there anything in which we can assist or comfort you?'

'Alas, noble sir,' answered the farmer, with the tears streaming down his face, 'no mortal man may help us. In the morning the terrible Giant Skrymsli is coming for our darling youngest son Rogner whom he has chosen for his dinner tomorrow, and though we have begged and prayed for mercy, nothing will persuade him to spare our beloved child.'

'This must never be!' cried Odin, springing to his feet, and letting fall his disguise. 'Tomorrow the boy shall be hidden safely from Skrymsli – and if I cannot hide him, then Honir my brother shall do so!'

Then, while the farmer and his wife knelt before the three Æsir, Odin strode to the door and, holding out his arms, began to chant great rolling Runes which he had learnt from Mimir his uncle, the wise Giant.

As he chanted the corn grew over many a wide acre, till, when the sun rose, as far as the eye could see there stretched a great golden harvest ripe for the sickle.

Then Odin took the boy Rogner and hid him in a single grain of corn in one ear on one straw in the midst of the great cornfield. Then the three Æsir stood in the doorway of the farmhouse to see what would happen, and before long the huge Giant came striding down from the mountains.

'Give me the boy Rogner!' cried Skrymsli.

'He is hiding in the cornfield,' said the farmer.

'Then I shall find him before sunset,' answered the Giant, and drawing his sharp sword he began to reap the corn with it, shaking each sheaf as he gathered it and flinging it aside until he had built a high stack at the end of the field.

Evening was falling as Skrymsli cut the fatal stalk of corn, shook the grains into his hand, and picked out the very one in which Rogner was hidden.

In his terror the child called to Odin for help, and one of his ravens flew down, snatched the grain out of Skrymsli's hand, and carried it to the farmhouse, where at once Rogner regained his own shape and size.

'I have done all I can to help you,' said Odin to the farmer. 'The sun has set, Skrymsli has gone, and the boy is safe.'

That night the three Æsir remained in the farmhouse, and in the morning they saw the Giant Skrymsli striding towards them again. Then Honir took Rogner's hand and led him quickly out by the back door and into a wood where two silvery-white swans flew down, and Honir changed the boy into a tiny feather on the neck of one of them.

Meanwhile the Giant had come to the farmhouse door.

'Give me the boy Rogner!' he cried.

'He is hiding in the greenwood,' said the farmer.

'Then I shall find him before sunset,' answered Skrymsli, and away he went into the wood.

All day he searched among the birds and the beasts who dwelt there, and in the evening he caught the very swan on whose neck Rogner was hidden. With a shout of triumph he raised the bird to his lips and bit at it. But Honir was watching, and sent a gust of wind which blew the feather away from the Giant's lips and carried it to the farmhouse, where the terrified boy became himself again.

'I have done all I can to help you,' said Honir to the farmer. 'The sun has set, Skrymsli has gone, and the boy is safe.'

Yet the three Æsir tarried still another night in the farmhouse, and next morning they saw the Giant Skrymsli striding towards them once more.

This time Loki took Rogner's hand and led him quickly out by the back door and down to the sea-shore. He set him in a boat, rowed out to sea, and casting his line soon caught three flounders. He hid the boy in the tiniest egg in the roe of one of them, and threw the three fishes overboard.

Meanwhile the Giant had come to the farm-house door.

'Give me the boy Rogner!' he cried.

'He has gone out fishing,' said the farmer.

'Then I shall find him before sunset,' answered Skrymsli, and away he went down to the sea-shore, where he got into his boat and rowed out from land. When he reached deep water he met Loki, who instantly steered his own boat so that Skrymsli's crashed into it and sank it.

Loki climbed into the Giant's boat, and sat shivering in the stern, begging Skrymsli to take him back to the shore before he died of cold.

But Skrymsli ignored him and rowed on until he was well out to sea, and there he anchored and cast his line.

Very soon he caught three flounders, and amongst them Loki recognized the fish in which he had hidden Rogner.

'Good master Giant,' begged Loki, 'give me that little fish. There's nothing like raw fish for a man who's just been half-drowned.'

'So you're hungry, are you?' growled Skrymsli, picking up the fish. 'Well, I am afraid you will have to wait until sunset!'

With that he opened the three fishes and counted every egg in their roes until he came to the one in which Rogner was hidden.

But Loki was watching carefully, and the moment he saw that Skrymsli had the egg he turned himself into a falcon, snatched it from the Giant's hand, and flew with it to the shore.

There he turned Rogner back into his own shape and size and said to him:

'Wait where you are until the Giant actually sets foot on shore, then run your fastest across that stretch of very white sand and put up this iron pole at the far end of it.'

Rogner did as he was told, and the sand seemed to move and whistle strangely beneath his feet as he sped across. But when he had turned and stuck in the iron pole as he had been instructed, he saw that the Giant was sinking in the sand.

Down went Skrymsli to his knees, and then with a tremendous effort and a fearful roar of rage, he dragged out one leg and plunged forward. He tripped and fell, and put out his hands to save himself. But both his hands and arms went down into the quicksand as though it had been water, and he struck his head so hard on the iron pole that he knocked himself unconscious. Before he could recover his wits, he had gone down head first into the quicksand and was smothered. Only his legs stuck up out of the ground, and Loki came along with the Giant's own sharp reaping hook and cut them both off.

After Loki had dealt so successfully with Skrymsli, Odin and the other Æsir were still more inclined to take his advice in matters concerning Giants – and very soon his cunning was again put to the test, but in a far more serious matter.

This time it was not merely a farmer's son, but the very existence of Asgard which was in danger. It happened that Odin and the other Æsir were met in council to decide how to build a wall round Asgard to be a sure defence against their enemies.

While they were discussing the difficulties of this undertaking, Heimdall, the guardian of the Bridge Bifrost, came to them and said:

'Father Odin, there stands a man in the plain below the gate of Asgard who offers to build a wall that shall keep out both the Hill Giants and the Rime Giants. But he would speak with you all and make a bargain over the price you are to pay for his labours.'

So Odin and the other Æsir came to the gate of Asgard and looked down to where the man stood, his arm through the reins of a fine white stallion. He was tall and grim-looking, but there seemed to be nothing unusual about him, except that he was in an exceedingly bad temper.

'Are you the master mason who offers to build our wall?' asked Odin.

'I am,' answered the man. 'And I swear to build the whole wall in three years, strong enough and high enough to keep out all the Giant race.'

'And what is your price for doing so great a feat of building?' asked Odin.

'Your solemn oath to give me Freya, Lady of the Vanir, as my bride,' answered the man, 'as well as the Sun and the Moon.'

When the Æsir heard this, they were about to treat it as a joke and send the man away with a warning against such impudence.

But Loki said: 'Perhaps there is more to this. You know very well that none of us could build such a wall in three years. It is not possible that a man should either, but he may know some craft which we lack. So agree to his terms, but insist that he must build the wall to the very last stone in one winter, with no one to help him, and that if on the first day of summer any part of the work remains undone, he will receive no wages ... He cannot possibly complete it, but he may at least lay a good foundation, which we shall get for nothing.'

It seemed as if Loki had drunk of Kvasir's Blood, for the Æsir were persuaded by his words, and Odin proposed the conditions to the man.

'To all this will I agree,' he replied, 'and no man shall help me. But you must allow me to use my horse here.'

There seemed no harm in this, so all the Æsir swore solemn oaths to give him Freya, with the Sun and the Moon, if the work were completed by the first day of summer.

The next day was the beginning of winter, and the strange mason set to work. By nightfall the watching Æsir were already feeling uneasy, for the mason's horse Svadilfari carried and hauled such amazing quantities of such huge stones that it seemed little short of miraculous. Moreover the mason himself squared every one of those stones before morning and set each in position, firmly mortared to the next.

So the work went on. Every day Svadilfari hauled vast loads of stone, and night after night his master built them up until, as winter drew towards an end, the wall was nearing completion.

Then the Æsir met in council once more, in a great state of alarm and consternation.

'It is only three days until the beginning of summer,' said Odin, 'and you can all see that this mason will easily finish the wall by then. Shall we therefore be obliged to give one of our number, Freya the Beautiful, to a stranger from Midgard? And must we destroy both Midgard and Asgard by losing the Sun and the Moon – which this wizard may sell to the Giants our enemies?'

'But we have sworn an oath – we cannot break that,' the son of bright Baldur, Forseti the Oath-keeper, reminded him.

'Why did we ever swear so foolish – so wicked

an oath?' asked Tyr, the War-lord, angrily. 'We could have fought the Giants without a wall!'

'We were persuaded to it by cunning Loki,' said Odin slowly.

'You all agreed that what this mason offered was an impossible boast,' Loki reminded the Æsir. 'You must not blame me for what was only a suggestion – which you were quite ready to follow.'

'I was not here,' grumbled Thor, his red beard bristling. 'I was away guarding against Giants. And I'm certain Loki, the son of Laufey, tricked you. He got us into this trouble, he must get us out of it – or he'll have me to reckon with.'

Most of the Æsir seemed to agree with Thor, and Loki began to feel frightened. 'I had no more idea than you that the man's horse had magic powers,' he protested. 'I'm sure I can think of a way to prevent the mason from earning his prize – my mind is full of schemes. But it pains me to think that you suspect me of bringing this terrible danger upon us by anything but the merest accident.'

'No one distrusts you, Loki,' answered Odin. 'You are one of us, and my brother by blood. But Thor is right: in you there is more cunning than any of us possess. You advised us to make this bargain – and you must save us from having to keep it.'

'But without breaking our oath or staining our honour,' murmured Forseti. And to this the Æsir agreed, and the council broke up.

Loki at once went away out of Asgard by himself and Thor muttered suspiciously that he was taking refuge with the Giants, and that Heimdall the Watchman of Asgard should not have let him cross Bifrost.

But the other Æsir said nothing: only they took their places on the almost completed wall and looked down to see what would happen.

As night fell the mason arrived leading the great stallion Svadilfari with another load of stones. They had almost reached the foot of the wall, when suddenly, out of a little wood nearby, sprang another horse, a beautiful white mare, neighing and prancing.

At once Svadilfari seemed to go mad. He reared up, neighing in answer to the white mare, and with a sudden plunge broke his traces, oversetting the load of stones, and dashed away into the darkness.

All that night and all the next day Svadilfari followed the white mare, and Svadilfari's master followed him, shouting and cursing in vain. But on the last night of winter he came limping back to Asgard without his horse.

Over Bifrost he strode, and stood in the midst of the Æsir, and cursed them as cheats and oath-breakers. Greater and greater grew his fury; until suddenly it overcame all his cunning, and he grew greater too, huger and uglier and more evil. Then the Æsir knew him for one of their enemies the Rime Giants from Jotunheim, and they gathered round him angry and threatening.

But Odin in his wisdom placed the shield Svalin in the eastern sky to hide the rising sun. Suddenly the Giant paused in his threats of tearing down Asgard and casting the Æsir except Freya into Nifelheim, and with a cry of dismay he sprang up on to his new wall for he had seen the sun shining round the edge of the shield.

Then Odin cast down Svalin, and the risen sun shone on the Giant and turned him into a stone, which tipped forward off the wall, fell down, down to the plain of Midgard far below, and broke into a mass of splinters.

But Loki came back to Asgard some months later leading the wonderful grey horse Sleipnir, the fastest horse in the world, which had eight legs. It was the foal of Svadilfari and the white mare, and it became Odin's horse and bore him ever afterwards through the clouds and over Midgard, wherever he had a mind to go.

5

LOKI MAKES MISCHIEF

After the adventure of the Giant mason a change seemed to come over Loki. His cunning grew unkinder; his gay impudence seemed often to be slyness; and he spent more and more of his time away from Asgard.

Wise Odin saw the change in him, and was troubled. For already he understood enough of the future to know that one of the Æsir was destined to prove a traitor. And who more likely than Loki, who had been born a Giant?

Odin sat upon Lidskialf, his high throne above Asgard, and looked down upon all the worlds.

Suddenly in distant Jotunheim he saw Loki playing with three monsters in the courtyard of a dark
castle.

Swiftly he sent for Hermodur his son, the messenger of the Æsir:

'Go straightway to Jotunheim,' he commanded.
'Loki our companion has forgotten that he is one
of the Æsir and is dwelling in the castle of Angurboda the Giantess. Bid him come to me without
delay.'

Swift as light Hermodur sprang away, leapt
upon Sleipnir, Odin's eight-legged horse, and was
gone.

Very soon Loki stood before Odin in the groves
of Asgard, an impudent smile on his lips, but fear
lurking in his eyes.

'No, I do not forget that I am of the Æsir, nor
that the Giants are deadly foes to us,' said Loki,
when Odin had spoken of what he had seen. 'But
remember, your mother Bestla was of that race –
and she was my father's cousin . . . We Æsir can
mingle with the Giants without taking their side.
And it chanced when I led the horse Svadilfari
into Jotunheim, and so saved Asgard from the
Giant who would have taken Freya, the Sun, and
the Moon in spite of all that any of you could do –
it happened that I saw the most lovely of all the
Giant race, fair Angurboda. I loved her, she loved
me – we are married, and three strange children
have been born to us.'

'It is not right that the Æsir should wed with

the Giants and have monsters for children –' began Odin.

'Indeed,' sneered Loki. 'Yet you, Allfather of Asgard and Midgard, once wedded Jord. Were not Anar her father and Nott her mother both of the Giant race? And is her son and yours – is great Thor a monster?'

'Loki, you speak of things which you do not understand,' said Odin. 'It was only in obedience to the wisdom of Mimir, and to the will of the Norns, that I wedded kindly Jord, the Earth-Giantess, in the faraway days when the world was still in the making. Without Thor, we could not have stood against the Giants, as well you know. Thor came as our protection, but I very much fear that these children of yours are born to destroy us.'

Then Odin commanded his sons to bring the children of Loki to Asgard, and they set out for Jotunheim with Thor and Tyr in the lead.

When they returned, they led with them such monsters that the queens of the Æsir, Frigga and Sif, Iduna and lovely Freya, might well turn pale at the sight of them.

For the youngest was Hela, with one half of her body living, human flesh, and the other half the livid hue of decay. The second was the great serpent Jormungand, rising like a twisted pillar of evil. And the eldest was the Fenris Wolf – the biggest and the fiercest of all wolves.

'These I may not slay,' said Odin, 'for the

course of fate cannot be broken, and the web of the Norns once woven cannot be unpicked. But go, Hela, daughter of Loki, and find your own realm below Nifelheim: to you shall come the spirits of the dead who do not fall in battle. Across the River Gioll they must go – the river that none may cross again – and there Garm of the Bloody Breast, the watchdog of Helheim, shall guard your grey domains. Go, Queen of the Dead!'

Odin stretched out his hand, and with a bitter cry Hela sank through the earth, down to the lowest world, there to reign until Ragnarok, the Day of the Last Great Battle, shall dawn.

Next Odin took Jormungand and flung him into the sea; and there he grew and grew until he encircled the earth, and held his tail in his mouth; and there, as the Midgard Serpent, he too is fated to remain until the Day of Ragnarok.

But the Fenris Wolf was kept in Asgard, though only Tyr dared go near him each day to give him meat.

He grew and grew, however, and became more and more dangerous. And Odin learnt from Mimir's Head that this Wolf was destined to be their destruction. He knew that he might not kill him, so now he called the Æsir together once more, and set out the case.

'Leave him to me!' muttered Thor. 'I shall see whether we can kill him or not!'

'It must not be,' said Odin firmly. 'He is the child of one of us, and to slay any in Asgard would bring the Day of Ragnarok upon us more swiftly than anything which the Giants could do.'

'Then let us take him away and tie him up with a chain which he cannot break,' said Thor. And this they decided to do.

So they made a very strong chain called Laeding, and took it and showed it to the Wolf.

'You are so strong,' said Tyr. 'Suppose you try and see if you can break this chain!'

The Fenris Wolf looked at Laeding, and curled up his lips in a snarl of contempt.

'Bind me if you wish,' he growled scornfully.

So they fastened Laeding round him, linked the ends together, and stood back to watch.

Fenris rose, shook himself, and stretched lazily – and the chain Laeding broke into small pieces that fell tinkling to the ground.

After this the Æsir laboured long and carefully making another and far stronger chain, while Fenris howled in the courtyard of Asgard and grew mightier day by day.

When the second chain, the chain Dromi, was finished, Tyr took it and showed it to Fenris, and the Wolf grinned wickedly when he saw it.

'You broke Laeding so easily,' said Tyr, 'that we feel you have not had a real trial of strength. But now we have put all our skill into making this chain. See if you can escape from Dromi as easily as you did from Laeding.'

Fenris examined Dromi, and saw that it was very strong and heavy.

'It will be a little harder,' he said. 'But bind me up, and I'll dash out of Dromi as surely as I lashed out of Laeding. I have grown in strength since my first feat!'

So the Æsir gathered in the courtyard, and once again the Fenris Wolf was bound in chains as securely as Thor and Tyr could make them.

This time he strained and struggled in the iron grip of Dromi, beat it against the stone pavement and stretched his hardest. In the end it flew into fragments as Laeding had done, and he cried exultantly:

'See! I have indeed dashed out of Dromi! What are your puny chains to me? But I am tired of this sport. You cannot find a chain to hold me, so trouble me no more with any such nonsense.'

Fenris went to his dinner, stuffed himself with raw meat, and lay down contentedly – rejoicing to see from his shadow that he was still growing.

The Æsir, however, met again in council, and even Thor looked grave. But wise Frey rose up and said:

'It is evident that none of the Æsir, nor of the Vanir, can make a chain strong enough to hold the Fenris Wolf. And if we cannot, no man in Midgard can either; and I doubt whether any Giant in Jotunheim could do it.'

'Let us have no more dealings with Giants,' muttered Thor. 'A Giant smith might be just as dangerous as a Giant mason was!'

'No, I would not counsel any help out of

Jotunheim,' said Frey. 'But let me now send my faithful messenger Skirnir to the land beyond Nifelheim, to Svartalfheim, the home of the Black Elves. There dwell certain Dwarfs who are more skilled in the forging of chains than any in all the Nine Worlds.'

The Æsir agreed to this, and Skirnir the messenger set forth.

When he returned he carried with him a grey chain of tiny links which was as soft and smooth as a silken ribbon: and he carried it easily in one hand.

'This is the chain Gleipnir,' he said as he handed it to Frey. 'The Dwarfs swore to me that it alone could hold the Fenris Wolf, and that he would not break from it until the day of Ragnarok, when all bonds will be broken.'

'The chain looks thin and weak,' mused Odin, letting it run through his fingers.

'It is a magic chain, made with the aid of many spells,' answered Skirnir. 'Six things went to its making, so the Dwarfs bade me say: the sound of a cat's foot-fall, the beard of a woman, the roots of a rock, the sinews of a bear, the breath of a fish, and the spittle of a bird. And indeed you may now perceive that a cat's foot-fall no longer makes a sound, women now have no beards, and you cannot find the roots of a rock: as for the other things I have not yet put them to the test.'

So Odin slipped the chain into his pouch, and he and most of the Æsir went down into the yard where the Fenris Wolf lived.

The great creature came yawning and stretching out into the sunlight when they called him, and all noticed how much larger he had grown since the day on which he had broken the chain Dromi.

'Come hunting with us in the forests of Midgard,' said Tyr.

'Not so,' answered the Wolf. 'I do not leave Asgard – yet. Here I know that I am safe.'

'Well, then, come across the plains of Asgard,' said Tyr. 'Though there we are not so likely to find game.'

Fenris readily agreed to this, and they set off through the bright woods and meadows until they came to the Lake of Amsvartnir. In the middle of this was a rocky island, and at Uller's suggestion they crossed to it.

'I have shot many a long-horned deer here,' said the Bowman of Asgard as they landed. 'So we should have good hunting.'

When they sat down to eat and rest a few hours later, Odin drew out the chain Gleipnir.

'I have a wonder here,' he said to the Æsir, as well as to Fenris. 'It is a chain as light as silk, and yet I cannot break it.'

The other Æsir took it one by one, and even Thor found that it was too strong for him.

'But Fenris could break it,' he said. 'If he could dash out of Dromi as he did, this little thing would cause him no trouble.'

Fenris sniffed at the chain Gleipnir, and curled up his nose suspiciously.

'It will not add to my glory, to snap so thin a chain,' he growled. 'And if there is anything of enchantment and dark magic about it, I swear it shall never be bound about me.'

'Surely you could easily break such a silken band,' said Thor. 'And if not – well, the Æsir will know that you are only an ordinary weak Wolf, and even our wives will no longer be afraid of you. If we have nothing to fear from you, why should we not unbind you?'

'If you bind me and I find I cannot get free again,' growled Fenris, 'it will be too late, if you mean to cheat me . . . No, I refuse to be bound with the chain Gleipnir . . . Yet I hate to think that you may doubt my courage. So if one of you will place his hand in my mouth as a pledge of good faith, you may bind me with Gleipnir.'

The Æsir turned pale and looked askance at one another, for nobody liked to accept the Wolf's challenge.

But brave Tyr stepped forward.

'Wolf Fenris,' he cried. 'I am not afraid! See, I place my hand between your jaws. Now let Thor and the rest fasten the fetters and the chain upon you.'

Fenris stood still while Gleipnir was fastened round him, with fetters linked into place round his paws. Then he stretched himself and lashed out: but as he did the chain seemed to grow hard and tight, and the more he struggled the tighter and the harder it grew.

Then all the Æsir laughed with joy and relief – all except brave Tyr, for he had lost his hand.

They drew the chain through a solid rock, when they saw that the Wolf was truly bound and unable to break loose, and they pegged the end of it with a great splinter of stone driven far into the earth.

Fenris thrashed about him, howling terribly and trying to bite, so Thor placed a sword in his mouth with the guards caught in his lower jaw and the point piercing up into the roof, and that served as a gag.

'There he shall lie bound,' said Odin solemnly, 'until the Day of Ragnarok – and then only shall he break loose. Here in Asgard we could not slay him, for the place is holy and no life blood of the Æsir or their kin may be shed amongst us.'

Then the Æsir went back to the high halls of Asgard, and that night they feasted in Valhalla with light hearts.

But Loki, although he feasted as merrily as the rest, and drank great horns of mead to the over-throw of the Giants, to the bravery of one-handed Tyr, and to the might of Thor the Thunderer, could not forgive the Æsir for what they had done, nor for banishing Angurboda to the depths of Helheim and giving him back his true wife Sigyn whom he had deserted for the Giantess.

But his anger was fiercest against Thor, who had actually bound Fenris, and who, as he quaffed the strong mead from his horn, boasted of what he had done and of his hatred for all Giants and all who made friends with them.

Loki said nothing. Indeed he laughed heartily at Thor's taunts and jests. But he slipped away from the feast while it was still dark night, bent on mischief and revenge.

In the morning when Thor strode home to his great palace of Bilskirnir, the Storm-Serene, his beautiful wife Sif met him in tears, with a cloak muffled tightly round her face.

'What has chanced?' cried Thor, his eyes flashing.

Weeping and with eyes downcast in shame, Sif slowly drew back the cloak and let it fall.

Then Thor cried out in grief and rage, for all her lovely golden hair had gone, and her head was as bald as the stubbly cornfield after the harvest has been gathered in.

'A thief came in the night while I slept,' she sobbed. 'When I woke this morning all had gone – all, all.'

Then Thor strode through Asgard, his eyes flashing like lightning, his red beard bristling with rage, roaring with fury until the thunder rolled upon the hills of Midgard and distant Jotunheim.

'Loki, son of Laufey!' bellowed Thor. 'Where is that spawn of the Giants? He alone could have done this thing. Show me Loki the mischief-maker so that I may break every bone in his body!'

Loki had stayed in Asgard, thinking that no one would suspect him, and knowing that the Æsir would not allow any harm to befall him there. But when Thor grabbed hold of him, roaring that he would carry him to Jotunheim and there break him into little pieces, he grew frightened.

'Let me go,' he begged. 'I will make you any recompense you like. I was angry and did not think what I was doing.'

But Thor only shook him until his teeth rattled, and went striding across Asgard shouting:

'Unless you can put back the hair which you have cut off, so that it grows again upon Sif's head, I'll break your bones and crush you under a mountain, so that you can work no more mischief!'

'I will! I will!' cried Loki. 'Put me down, and listen to me.'

Thor set him on his feet doubtfully, but did not let go his hold.

'Well,' he growled, 'how will you replace the hair you have dared to cut from Sif's head?'

'The three Dwarfs who made the chain Gleipnir!' cried Loki eagerly. 'Those three sons of Ivaldi who live in Svartalfheim can make new hair if anyone can! Let me go to them, and I will also pay a fine for all the trouble I've caused. If you break my bones, Sif will never get her hair again; but if you let me go now to Svartalfheim there is every chance that she may. You will lose nothing by letting me try – but may lose everything if you don't.'

Slow-witted Thor took a little while to see this. But when he did he flung Loki from him, shouting:

'Go to Svartalfheim then, and do your best with the sons of Ivaldi. But don't think to escape me if you fail. Wherever you are, I'll find you!'

Loki picked himself up, muttering curses on Thor under his breath, and set out from Asgard towards the land of the Dark Elves.

Over the Bridge Bifrost he went, and through Midgard to the high, lonely mountains, in the gloomy caverns beneath which dwelt the Dwarfs and their cousins the Dark Elves.

Down into the caves went Loki, by winding passage and steep stair, until he heard in front of him the clink of hammers on anvils, and saw the red glow of the forges.

At last he came out into the cavernous under-world where the Dwarfs were at work, digging the gold, the iron, and the jewels from the rocks and working them into beautiful swords and cups and necklaces, armour, and other treasures.

Loki found the sons of Ivaldi, and when he had told them what he wanted, the master-craftsman, Dvalin, exclaimed:

'This will bring us great honour and glory among the Æsir! Let us set to work at once, my brothers, and show them how great is our skill.'

So they put gold into the fire, and began to work, while the bellows roared and the sparks flew up the chimney like the molten breath of a volcano.

And first clever Dvalin made the spear Gungnir as a gift for Odin. This is the best of all spears and never fails to hit its mark.

Next they made the ship Skidbladnir as a gift for Frey, lord of the winds. This is the best of all ships, for it can sail over land as well as sea, and through the air also, no matter which way the wind is blowing. It can carry all the Æsir, with their steeds, at one time! and yet fold up small enough to be carried in one hand or in a warrior's belt.

Last of all Dvalin spun golden thread finer than ever was drawn from a mortal spinning-wheel, and made from it new hair for Sif.

'If this is placed on her head,' he told Loki, 'it will grow there at once just as her own hair did. And I have put into it a charm so that it may never again be stolen by force or cunning.'

Loki was delighted, and certain that he was safe now from Thor's vengeance and the anger of the Æsir.

'You are the greatest of all smiths,' he cried to Dvalin. 'Not in Midgard nor in Asgard, nor even here and among the Black Dwarfs, is there any other who could fashion such cunning, such wondrous gifts for the Æsir.'

Now it chanced that another Dwarf named Brok heard Loki's words, and he sprang up in a great rage.

'That is not true!' he shrieked. 'My brother Sindri is a far better smith than Dvalin. I'll wager my head on it!'

'I'll take your wager!' cried Loki indignantly. 'My head against yours that Sindri cannot make three gifts for the Æsir rarer and more wonderful than Dvalin's.'

'Good,' answered Brok, grinning evilly. 'I shall be cutting off your head before night . . . I must ask Sindri to make me a special weapon for that purpose!'

Then Brok led the way to Sindri's smithy, and the Dwarf smith grinned and nodded when he heard of the bet.

'Yes, yes!' he cried. 'I'll do better than Dvalin, son of Ivaldi, ever did. Gungnir, Skidbladnir, and hair for Sif! Bah, wait till you've seen my gifts for the Æsir!'

Then Sindri mingled his metals and poured in his charms. When this was done he set a pig-skin bellows on the hearth, and told Brok to blow until he came back.

'Blow hard,' he instructed his brother, 'and do not cease for a moment – no, not even to mop your brow – not even to draw breath: for if you pause for anything whatsoever, that which lies in the fire will be spoilt.'

Then he went into another cave, while Brok blew at the bellows. But Loki, with a sly look in his eyes, stole quietly out of the smithy in the opposite direction.

Presently, as Brok worked at the bellows, a gadfly came and stung him on the hand until the blood came, but Brok never even paused to dash it away.

Sindri came back a few minutes later and drew

from the fire a boar with golden bristles and mane of gleaming gold.

'Good,' said he. 'Gullinbusti is complete. Now blow at the bellows again, and do not stop for a moment, or my next work will be spoilt.'

With that he laid more gold in the hearth, and went out of the smithy again. Presently as Brok toiled at the bellows the gadfly came again and stung him on the neck until the blood came. But Brok never even paused to dash it away.

Sindri came back a few minutes later and drew from the fire a glimmering ring of gold.

'Good,' said he, 'Draupnir is complete. Now work at the bellows again, and do not stop for a moment, or my last and greatest work will be spoilt.'

With that he laid a great mass of iron in the hearth, and went out of the smithy again.

Presently as Brok worked at the bellows the gadfly came once more and stung him on the eyelid until the blood came. Then Brok grabbed at the gadfly as swiftly as he could and swept it from him and dashed the blood out of his eye. But the bellows grew flat for a moment as he did so, although a moment later he was working away at them as hard as ever.

Sindri came back and drew from the fire a great iron hammer.

'Alas,' said he, 'Miolnir came near to being spoilt. See, it is a little too short in the handle. Yet even so I am certain that you will win your wager, brother Brok. So take our three gifts, and hasten to Asgard to lay them before the Æsir for their judgement.'

Loki had come back to the smithy in his own form by this time, and he looked scornfully at Brok's gifts, though already he was beginning to feel anxious about which the Æsir would consider the best.

However, he set out for Asgard with Dvalin and Brok, and when they arrived the Æsir assembled and Loki explained the presence of the two Dwarfs by telling of the wager.

Then Odin, Thor, and Frey sat down in the seats of judgement, and Loki advanced with Dvalin behind him.

First Thor took the hair and set it upon Sif's head. And immediately it grew there as if it had never been lost, and she tossed back her head and smiled once more like the bright earth when summer returns after the bareness and cold of winter.

Then Loki handed the spear Gungnir to Odin, explaining how it could never miss its aim, nor be stopped in its thrust, whatever came in its way. And finally he gave the ship Skidbladnir to Frey telling him how it would speed over land or sea with a favourable breeze as soon as the sail was raised, yet could be folded like a napkin and thrust into his best.

The three Æsir admired their gifts, and Odin said:

'Dwarf Brok, it will indeed be hard for you to surpass these three, for never before did I behold such workmanship.'

Brok, however, stepped forward with a confident bow; and first of all he gave to Odin the ring Draupnir.

'There, my lord, is the gift of greatest wealth,' he said. 'Keep that ring well, and on every ninth night shall fall from it eight rings of equal value.'

Then he gave to Frey the boar Gullinbusti, saying:

'There, my lord, is the gift of greatest speed. Keep this boar well, for he can run through air or water better than any horse. Moreover, such a glow of light comes from his mane and bristles that you can never be lost in the dark, even though you pass through deepest Nifelheim itself.'

Last of all he gave to Thor the hammer Miolnir, and said:

'There, my lord, is the gift of greatest strength. Keep this hammer well, for it shall never fail you. You may smite with it as hard as you will and break whatever you hit. And if you throw it at anything, it will hit that at which you fling it, and return to your hand however far it goes. Yet it is so small that you may carry it in your belt. But I must tell you that there is one flaw in its making: the handle is a trifle short.'

After this the three Æsir discussed the gifts among themselves, and then Odin gave judgement:

'We feel,' he said, 'that the hammer Miolnir is the most precious of all these works, since in it is the greatest defence we have against the Giants our deadly enemies. Therefore we give this sentence: the Dwarf Brok has won his wager, and Loki must lose his head.'

'If you want my head, you must take it!' cried Loki with desperate bravado, and in an instant he was far away, leaping through the air on his shoes of swiftness.

'I'll bring him for you!' shouted Thor, and in a moment he had leapt into his chariot drawn by the two goats Gaptooth and Cracktooth and was whirling away across Midgard in a huge black thundercloud.

Before long he was back again and flung Loki out of the chariot on to the stone floor of Valhalla.

'There!' he cried, as the thunder rolled away in the distance. 'Now, Dwarf Brok, you may exact the penalty.'

Brok at once produced a sharp axe and advanced gleefully upon his victim.

'One moment!' exclaimed Loki, and the Dwarf paused. 'I readily admit that you have won the wager, and my head is forfeit. But will you not allow me to buy it back from you – which I would far rather do before you cut it off than afterwards, when it would be of little value to me?'

'No,' cried Brok. 'You have nothing to offer which I value. We have far greater treasures of rings and gold and weapons in Svartalfheim than

all you Æsir have, with the wealth of Midgard
and Jotunheim added. And that is all we Dwarfs
care about – except revenge . . . That gadfly which
stung me as I blew the bellows was remarkably
like you, crafty Loki. But this time your cunning
shall avail you nothing.'

'Yes, I confess myself beaten,' sighed Loki. 'So
if you will not spare me my head, you must come
and cut it off. Here I stand waiting for you to strike
. . . But of course you will remember that it was
only my head that I wagered: that belongs to you,
certainly – but my neck is still my own. So be very
careful when you cut off my head that you do not
touch my neck, for every scrap of it is mine, and I
forbid you to touch it . . . And of course when I
wagered my head, I meant the whole of it, so you
must take it all in one piece and leave none behind.'

There were a few moments of silence; and then
a great gust of laughter swept through Valhalla,
while Brok stood swinging his axe and looking
extremely foolish.

'I will not cut off your head,' he said at length.
'But just to warn you against boasting in future,
I'll sew your lips together . . . You talk far too
much, as I am sure these noble Æsir will agree,
and a little silence will do you no harm.'

Loki agreed thankfully to this, for it was a small
matter compared with the loss of his head.

'If your skill as a tailor is as great as your skill
as a smith,' he said, 'you'll sew a seam that I shall
be proud to wear across my face.'

So Brok set to work, but found that his sword was too blunt and clumsy to pierce the flesh of one of the Æsir.

'I wish I had my brother Sindri's awl here!' he cried.

Even as he said the words, Sindri's awl appeared suddenly, piercing Loki's lips, and Brok made the holes without any difficulty and laced them together with a thong.

Then all the Æsir laughed at Loki standing dumbly there without one of his usual jests to throw at them.

'Take a horn of mead with us, Loki!' they cried. 'Sing to us, Loki – sing a rousing catch of love or battle! Tell us some tale of your triumphs over your enemies!'

Loki endured all this mockery with downcast eyes; and when the Æsir were tired of their sport, and the two Dwarfs had departed from Asgard, he went quietly to his own palace and tore away the thong.

But ever afterwards his lips were scarred and uneven, and his smile was wicked where it had been only cunning before.

6

FREYA THE BRIDE

Frey and Freya, the Vanir children of Niord and
Skadi, grew up happily in Asgard, his chosen
place being among the Light Elves, and hers
among the young dwellers in Midgard – youths
and maidens who for the first time were knowing
the joys and sorrows of love.

Freya herself knew well both these joys and
these sorrows, for she was wedded to the handsome Odur whom she loved truly. They dwelt in
the halls and gardens of Asgard, and Folkvanger
was the name of their home. To it came certain of
the heroes of Midgard who had fallen in battle,

for Odin allowed her to choose from those whom the Valkyries brought to Valhalla which she would have in her domain.

In Folkvanger Freya and Odur lived happily for long, and they had two lovely daughters as fair as jewels, whose joy was in all beautiful things.

But a great sadness came to Freya, all the more sad because it was her own fault – though she never thought that her love of jewels could harm her happiness with Odur.

It happened that Freya wandered through Midgard and through Alfheim where her brother Frey ruled, and she came to the borders of Svartalfheim where the Black Dwarfs lived.

There Dvalin and his three brothers laid a trap for her. They set up their forge in the opening of a wide cave and made the most wonderful necklace of gold that was ever seen: and it was called Brisingamen, the Brising Necklace.

Freya stopped when she saw the Dwarfs, and caught her breath at the beauty of the necklace. Then she stood for a while watching them at their work, until the necklace was finished.

'Will you sell me that necklace for a treasure of silver?' she asked. 'For indeed I have never seen a fairer one, and I cannot live without it.'

'No,' answered the Dwarfs, 'all the silver in the world would not buy from us the Brisingamen.'

'Will you sell it to me for a treasure of gold?' asked Freya.

'No,' answered the Dwarfs. 'All the gold in the world would not buy it from us.'

'Then is there any treasure in the world for which you would sell me that necklace?' asked Freya. 'For now that I have seen Brisingamen, life without it is not to be endured.'

'Oh yes,' answered the Dwarfs. 'There is a treasure for which we would sell Brisingamen. You must buy it from each of us. That treasure is your love. To each of us you must be wedded for a day and a night – for of such short space is a marriage among the Dwarfs of Svartalfheim – and then Brisingamen shall be yours.'

Then Freya, in her madness, forgot all but the shimmer and the gleam of the world's most lovely adornment, the Brisingamen, than which no fairer necklace has ever been seen. She forgot Odur her husband, she forgot her two fair daughters, she forgot that she was a queen among the Æsir.

'Yes,' she answered, as if in a dream, 'for Brisingamen I would even wed with such as you.'

So the four Dwarfish weddings were held in distant Svartalfheim, and none of the Æsir knew what was happening – none that is but Loki the mischief-maker who seemed always to know where evil was brewing.

When Freya came back to Asgard, and dwelt once more in her palace in Folkvanger, she was ashamed of what she had done and hid the Brisingamen from the sight of everyone. But alone in her bower, which no one could enter against her will, she would take out the necklace and feast her eyes on its gleaming beauty.

But Loki went to Odur and told him what he had seen and heard. Odur would not believe him, and he thought it shame even to mention to Freya what Loki had said.

'I do not even believe that she has this necklace called Brisingamen,' ended Odur. 'But if she has, and you can steal it from her and show it to me, I will believe your story, and my heart will be broken.'

'It will be very hard to steal it,' protested Loki. 'You know how closely the door of Freya's bower fits, and how firmly it is locked from within!'

'If you do not prove your lying tale by the only means which I can accept,' cried Odur, 'I shall know it is a lie, and Thor shall beat you into pulp with his hammer Miolnir.'

So Loki set out to steal the Brising Necklace. He came by night to Freya's bower, but found the door fast locked, and with all his cunning he could not open it. Then he turned himself into a fly and fluttered about all the locks and joints, and found there no hole at all. But at last, up near the gable top, he found one hole scarcely bigger than if it had been made with a needle: and with great difficulty he managed to wriggle through it. Then he looked carefully about the bower to see if anyone was awake, but the whole room, and the palace about it, seemed plunged in sleep.

Loki went to Freya's bed, and saw her there

asleep, with the Brisingamen round her neck. And he saw that the clasp of the necklace was under her, so that he could not unfasten it.

Then he turned himself into a flea and sat on her cheek and bit her. Freya half-woke up, turned over, and then fell asleep again. As soon as she was breathing peacefully Loki took on his own shape again, undid the clasp and drew off the necklace. He unlocked the door and stole out quietly.

He went straight to Odur, showed him the necklace and told him all that he had done.

Then in bitter grief Odur flung down the necklace and wandered out of Asgard, away into the mists of the distance.

Freya woke in the morning, found Brisingamen gone and the doors unlocked, and knew that her secret had been discovered. Weeping bitterly, she sent for Odur to tell him all and beg his forgiveness: but Odur was gone.

Then she confessed to Odin. 'I can never rest now,' she sobbed, 'until I find my beloved Odur and ask his pardon for the great wrong I have done him; and I shall follow him across the world until I do.'

'It shall be as you say,' answered Odin solemnly, 'and the evil which you have done for the sake of a golden trinket shall be forgiven you. But in memory of your sin I decree that you must wear ever the Brising Necklace to remind you of what has passed.'

'I no longer have the accursed thing,' sobbed Freya. 'The thief who entered my bower took it, as I told you.'

'Only Loki could have been that thief,' said Odin, and he summoned his son Heimdall, the Watchman of Asgard, and asked if he had seen Loki.

'Yes,' answered Heimdall, 'the son of Laufey passed across Bifrost early this morning, not long after Odur went out from Asgard. Odur I cannot see, but Loki, in the shape of a seal, is hiding by the rocks of Singastein.'

'Go, then,' commanded Odin, 'and take from him the necklace called Brisingamen which the Black Dwarfs made of late in Svartalfheim. Bring it and clasp it about the neck of Freya – and see to it that neither Loki nor any other takes it from her again.'

Swift as light Heimdall sped on his errand, and when he came to the rocks near Singastein he called aloud:

'Loki, son of Laufey, come forth and in your own shape! I know where you hide and in what form. Come forth, I say, for I bring you a message from Odin, lord of the Æsir.'

But Loki in the form of a seal hid down under the rocks at the bottom of the sea and laughed to himself.

But he did not laugh a moment later when Heimdall also turned into a seal and came speeding down through the green waters to attack him.

Fiercely the battle raged between the two seals, but in the end Heimdall had the better of it, and led Loki back to Asgard in a very bad temper, wearing his own form and carrying the Brising Necklace.

Then Freya fastened Brisingamen about her neck, and went forth into the world in search of Odur, wandering from land to land, and weeping as she went. And as she wept the tear-drops fell from her eyes and turned into drops of rich red gold.

For long she was absent from Asgard, and her brother Frey was sorely troubled as to what might have befallen her. He blamed Odin for sending her out on her wanderings, for Odin could have found Odur and brought him back, but it was his will that Freya should wander through the world teaching men and women the gentle ways of love.

At last Frey could bear it no longer. One day when Odin had gone to seek wisdom at Mimir's Well he stole up to the high seat of Lidskialf to steal a glimpse out over all worlds – which Odin alone might do.

He did not see Freya; but his eyes were caught and held by a brightness in the far north. He looked long and earnestly, and saw Gerda, daughter of Giant Gymir, most lovely of all the daughters of the Rime Giants. As she walked the air shone about her, and light seemed to gleam from her very arms. Then suddenly she went into her father's icy castle, and all the light in the world seemed to Frey to have gone out.

Slowly and sadly he went down from Lidskialf, punished for his presumption in daring to sit in Odin's seat. Back in his own palace he spoke never a word, he did not eat, nor drink, nor sleep: and no one dared speak to him, for he looked about him so fiercely.

Then Niord his father summoned wise Skirnir, Frey's faithful companion, and begged him to discover what had chanced.

'I will go to him,' answered Skirnir, 'and question him as you command. But I do not go willingly, for I expect only sharp answers.'

Skirnir went to where Frey sat alone, brooding on his sorrow, and spoke to him:

'Tell me, great Frey, captain of the Æsir, why you sit all day alone in your halls.'

'How can I tell the heaviness of my heart-sorrow?' answered Frey. 'The sun shines day by day, but it brings no joy to me.'

'Can your grief be so great that you may not even tell it to your friend?' asked Skirnir. 'Have you forgotten how close we were in the past when we grew up as boys together? Do you not trust me still?'

Frey was touched by his words, and told Skirnir what troubled him: 'In Gymirsgard I saw a maid walking, and her I love,' he ended. 'The very sky shone when she raised her lovely arms. And now she is dearer to me than ever maid was to man. But the Æsir and the Vanir will surely frown on my love, for she is of the race of the Giants.'

But Skirnir said: 'Give me a swift horse, and your magic sword that cuts whatever the edge touches, and I will win her for you.'

'I will indeed give you my horse,' answered Frey, 'and with it my magic sword that fights of itself if he is bold that bears it.'

Skirnir took the sword in his hand, sprang upon Frey's horse, and rode off into Jotunheim. 'Speed forward, good steed!' he cried. 'The ways are dark, and we must cross the misty hills into the land of the Rime Giants – but we shall get there in safety if we meet no Trolls on the way!'

At last they drew near to Gymir's castle, and there Skirnir saw a shepherd sitting on a hillside.

'Shepherd, sitting on the rocks and watching all the ways!' he cried. 'Tell me how I may come to speak with Gerda, lovely daughter of great Gymir.'

'Are you mad?' cried the shepherd. 'Or are you already but a ghost? Never can mortal win speech with Gymir's maiden daughter.'

'None of us must turn aside,' answered Skirnir. 'We must go forward on our journey whatever dangers await us. I shall die when die I must, and the Norns already know which day that is to be.'

Inside the castle Gerda heard the sound of horse's hooves as Skirnir leapt over the wall and clattered in the yard.

'What is that?' she asked. 'The very earth seems to be quaking and all the castle shakes.'

'A man on a great steed has leapt the wall into

the yard,' answered her handmaiden. 'He has got off his horse now, and has turned it loose to graze.'

'Go, bid him into the hall,' exclaimed Gerda, 'and serve him with clear mead . . . But my heart misgives me lest this stranger is he of whom the prophecy tells – that through him shall come the death of my dear brother Beli.'

In the great hall Skirnir bowed low as Gerda came to meet him, carrying in her hands a horn of mead.

'Which of the sons of the Æsir or of the wise Vanir are you?' she asked as she made him welcome. 'And how did you cross the wall which surrounds my father's castle?'

'I am none of the Æsir, nor the wise Vanir, nor even of the Elves,' answered Skirnir, 'though indeed I came alone over the wall to visit you. But see, I have here eleven apples of solid gold: these, beauteous Gerda, I will give you to purchase your favour so that you may call Frey, Lord of the Vanir, your best beloved of all living.'

'Your golden apples I will never take to buy my love for any living wight,' answered Gerda. 'Nor shall Frey and I ever call one another husband and wife.'

'Look on this sword,' cried Skirnir, drawing Frey's magic blade. 'I could hew off your head with it at a single stroke, if you would not come with me to be Frey's love.'

'Never will I endure to be driven to love,' said

Gerda. 'Yet I think that swords shall flash and grow dim with blood if you meet any of my kin.'

'Look yet again upon this sword,' said Skirnir in a low, thrilling voice. 'Look, and behold how it is marked with magic Runes. They are spells which shall bring a curse upon you, if you do not reward Frey's true love. If the spell is cast upon you, demons shall pinch you every day, even here in Jotunheim. Either you shall lack a husband, or a three-headed Troll shall be your lord: yes, Rimegrim the monster whose home is in the Glen of Corpses shall have you to wife. Your soul shall be smitten so that you pine as Frey is pining. Odin shall be wroth with you. Thor's anger shall be kindled against you, Frey himself shall grow to hate you ... See, I print upon you the magic Rune " ᚦ ": love shall fill you, but love shall destroy you, if you do not take pity upon Frey.'

Then all the anger went out of Gerda's eyes, and they grew suddenly tender.

'See,' she murmured, 'in this cup I drink to Frey. I did not think that I should ever come to love one of the Vanir ... Yet now it seems on a sudden that I do.'

'Give me further answer ere I ride back to Asgard,' said Skirnir. 'When and where will you meet with Niord's glorious son?'

'In the wood called Barri, the peaceful copse that he knows well,' answered Gerda. 'There I will wait for him three nights from now; and there we may be wedded.'

Then Skirnir leapt upon his horse and spurred towards Asgard, where Frey was waiting eagerly for him.

'Tell me quickly, Skirnir,' he cried. 'Tell me before you unsaddle your horse or even set foot to the ground, how did you fare in Jotunheim? What says fair Gerda to my love?'

'Barri is the name of a peaceful copse well known to both of you,' said Skirnir quietly. 'There, three nights from now, Gerda will wait for her love – there she will become the wife of Frey, Niord's noble son.'

'Ah!' sighed Frey, the happiness growing in his eyes. 'But one night is long, two nights are longer – how can I endure to wait for three? A month has often seemed to me shorter than even one of these nights of waiting!'

Nevertheless the endless nights were passed in due course, and Frey went to meet his love in the Wood of Barri.

On the way he found the Giant Beli waiting for him: 'Never while I live shall you marry my sister Gerda!' roared Beli. 'And now you shall die, for I see you have no sword.'

Then Frey missed the Sword of Sharpness which he had given to Skirnir – yet he did not miss it so sorely as he was fated to do when the Sons of Muspell came against him on the Day of Ragnarok. For, as Beli whirled his terrible club over his head, Frey stooped to avoid the blow, picked up the horn of a hart which lay upon the ground, and stabbed the Giant to the heart.

Then he went on his way to the wood Barri, and there Gerda met him, and loved him truly at sight.

And there the Æsir and Vanir gathered for the wedding; and Freya came leaning on the arm of kindly Odur, whom she had found at last and won his forgiveness for falling beneath the cunning spell of the four Dwarfs.

All was mirth and gaiety in that magic grove as they feasted through the warm summer night, while the nightingale sang in the thicket, and the swans chanted their mysterious chorus on the lake nearby.

And when the stars were paling, all lay down to sleep amongst the flowers and the soft grasses, while the brief darkness fell like a gentle coverlet over them.

Yet in that darkness evil moved.

Morning came, and Thor sprang to his feet with a shout of rage that roused the Æsir from their slumbers in a moment.

'My hammer Miolnir, terror of the Giants, has gone!' he roared. 'When I lay down to sleep it rested at my side, under my hand. Some cunning thief has stolen it from me in the darkness.'

They called Loki before them, half-suspecting him, half-anxious to seek his aid.

'Yes, I'll help you to find who has stolen Thor's hammer,' said Loki at once. 'But only if Freya will lend me her feather cloak. Without it I cannot find the hammer.'

'You shall have my feather cloak,' answered Freya. 'I would lend it to you even if it were made of gold and silver, so long as you find Thor's hammer for him.'

So Loki wrapped the feather cloak about him, and flew away into Jotunheim until he came to Thrymheim, the place of Noise, and there he found Thrym, king of the Noise Giants, sitting on a hillside plaiting golden leashes for his greyhounds and making trimmings for the manes of his horses.

'Greetings, Loki son of Laufey!' he cried. 'How goes it with the Æsir? How goes it with the Elves? Why have you come alone into Jotunheim?'

Then Loki answered humbly: 'It goes ill with the Æsir! It goes ill with the Elves. Thor's hammer is lost and they have sent me to seek it. Tell me where you have hidden it!'

Thrym, lord of the Giants, laughed aloud: 'Yes, I have hidden the Thunderer's hammer!' he shouted. 'I have hidden it eight miles deep under the earth. No one can ever find it, nor shall I bring it back unless the Æsir send me Freya the beautiful to be my wife.'

Then away flew Loki, the feather cloak flapping in the wind. Out of Jotunheim he went and came into Asgard. Thor met him at the gate, and the first words that he spoke were: 'What news do you bring me out of the sky? Speak quickly, have you found my hammer?'

'I have good news for you,' answered Loki.

'Thrym the Giant of Noise has your hammer. He has hidden it eight miles under the earth where no one can find it. But he will give it back to you if you bring Freya the beautiful to be his wife.'

In his eagerness to recover Miolnir, Thor thought of nothing else, and he rushed to Freya's palace and burst into her bower, shouting:

'Make ready, Freya! Take your bride's veil and come with me to Jotunheim, for Thrym the Giant is to be your husband!'

Then Freya sprang up in rage, and her fury was so great that the Brising Necklace round her throat burst open and fell to the ground.

'Surely you are mad, Thor of the Æsir!' she cried. 'Or do you mean to insult me by suggesting that I would willingly desert Odur my dear lord to be the bride of a Giant?'

At that Thor hung his great head for shame, and told Freya what had happened. So she came with him to the council of the Æsir where they were all gathered to decide how they could get back Thor's hammer – which was Asgard's surest defence against the Giants.

In the end it was not cunning Loki but far-seeing Heimdall who thought of a plan.

'Let us send a false Freya as wife to Thrym!' he suggested. 'Let us hide Thor's face in the bride's veil, set the Brising Necklace round his neck, and fasten brooches on his breast. With keys jingling from his girdle, a woman's dress falling below his knees and a hood over his head, the Giant will think that he has indeed got Freya – until it is too late.'

The Æsir applauded this suggestion, but Thor was furious.

'If I let myself be wrapped in a bride's veil,' he cried, 'and am seen dressed as a woman, the Æsir will never cease from taunting me.'

'Speak not so, great Thor,' said Loki, his eyes twinkling. 'But think how soon the Giants will dwell in Asgard if you do not get back your hammer.'

So Thor consented to do as Heimdall suggested. Very soon the bridal veil was wrapped over his face, the Brisingamen was hung about his neck, the keys jingled at his girdle, the dress fell about his knees, the brooches glimmered in the front of his bodice and the hood was wound neatly about his head.

Then Loki exclaimed: 'Thor, I will follow you and be your bridesmaid! We two will drive to Jotunheim together!'

So, when Loki was disguised in dress and veil and hood as well, Thor's chariot was brought out and his two goats Gaptooth and Cracktooth were harnessed to it. Then the false Freya and her falser maid got into it, shook the reins, and sped away over Midgard and into Jotunheim, the rocks splitting beneath their wheels, and sparks flying like lightning from the stones.

When Thrym the Giant saw the chariot drawing near to Thrymheim with the two veiled figures in it, he cried aloud:

'Rise up quickly, my Giants all, and make ready! Here comes Freya the daughter of Niord lord of the Vanir to be my wife. My stables are filled with gold-horned kine, and with black oxen that have never a spot or blemish, such as delight the Giant kind. I have treasures and jewels stored in my castle: all that I lacked was Freya the Beautiful!'

So the Bride and her Maid were welcomed to Thrymheim, and a mighty feast was prepared in the great hall of the castle.

But when the Bride ate for her share a whole ox, eight salmon, and all the dainties prepared for the ladies, besides drinking three casks of mead, Thrym looked at her suspiciously and exclaimed:

'Surely no bride was ever so hungry! I have never seen a girl take such big mouthfuls, nor drink such quantities of mead!'

The Bride did not know what to say, but fortunately the Bridesmaid was quick-witted, and found a ready answer:

'Freya has not eaten for eight days!' she piped. 'She was so eager to reach Jotunheim and be your bride that she could touch neither food nor drink.'

When the meal was ended, Thrym bent down to kiss the bride. But scarcely had he raised her veil, when he started back the whole length of the hall.

'Why are Freya's eyes so glaring?' he cried. 'It seems as if flames were darting from them.'

Once again the quick-witted bridesmaid found

a ready answer: 'Freya's eyes are red because she has not slept for eight nights, so eager was she to reach Jotunheim and be your bride.'

Then came in Thrym's sister and begged a gift of the bride: 'Give me a golden ring off your arm,' she cried.

But Thrym interrupted her. 'Time enough for that afterwards,' he exclaimed. 'Now let us on with the wedding. Bring in the hammer Miolnir which is the bride-price, and lay it in the bride's lap so that the wedding may go forward. Let us lay our hands together upon it and join them in the oath of wedlock.'

The heart of Thor laughed within him when he again felt Miolnir in his hands.

'Take this in token of wedlock from Freya the Bride!' he shouted, flinging off his disguise; and with one blow of his hammer he laid Thrym lifeless on the floor.

'And taste iron instead of gold!' he cried as he smote down the Giant's sister. Then he turned upon the rest of the Giants and slew them all with Miolnir, before he and Loki set out once more for Asgard.

When they arrived it was to find that Freya had nearly been lost while they were away, this time to Alviss the cunning Dwarf, who had learnt all about the theft of Miolnir and Giant Thrym's demand.

He had come to Asgard on the night before Thor's return, striding up Bifrost Bridge as if he were one of the Æsir.

'Take me to Odin!' he cried when Heimdall the Watchman challenged him. 'Take me at once! There is not a moment to be lost if you would save Asgard from the Giants: they are marching against you even now, and I come with a message to Odin.'

Heimdall took the Dwarf to where Odin sat, and the king of the Æsir questioned him as to who he was and how he dared to enter Asgard.

'I am Alviss, the all-wise,' answered the Dwarf. 'I dwell beneath the earth, my home is under the rock, and I have come to fetch Freya the Bride.'

'You are likely to be a sorry bridegroom,' answered Odin, 'indeed you look pale and corpse-like already, as if your home was among the dead.'

'Do not jest with me!' cried the Dwarf. 'Thor is a prisoner of Thrym the Giant, and the hosts of Jotunheim are marching on Asgard. But they will turn back if I bring Freya to be Thrym's bride indeed.'

'And why have they sent you?' asked Odin slowly. 'Are you a fit one to bring such a message?'

'Fit!' shrieked the Dwarf, 'I am Alviss the All-wise – the wisest of all the Dwarf-kind!'

'You must prove your wisdom, then,' said Odin gravely. 'Come, tell me, All-wise that you are, knowing the whole history of mankind, how are the Heavens named in every world?'

'Men speak of the Heavens,' answered Alviss,

eager to display his knowledge, 'the Æsir call it the Sky; the Vanir call it Wind-roof; it is Upheim to the Giants, while the Elves call it Fair-roof and the Dwarfs Drip-hall.'

'And how is Fire that burns all things called in each of the worlds?' asked Odin.

'It is called Fire among men,' answered the Dwarf, 'and Eild by the Æsir; to the Vanir it is Wave-flame, Consumer to the Giants, Furnace to the Dwarfs, and Destroyer to those in Hell.'

Twelve such questions Odin asked Alviss the Dwarf, but when he came to the thirteenth he said:

'Now tell me how Night the daughter of Narvi is called in each of the worlds.'

'Night among men,' cried the Dwarf, 'but Niol among the Æsir. It is Unlight to the Giants, but Sleep-joy to the Elves and Dream-fairy to the Dwarfs.'

'So much for Night,' cried Odin, 'and indeed you know many things, Alviss the Dwarf. But one thing you have forgotten. Night has ended: how do you call Day when you see it in Asgard?'

Then, as the sun rose and the first beams fell upon him, Alviss strove to answer. But no words came, nor did his lips move again: for he had turned into stone.

And with the new day came Thor and Loki back to Asgard with Miolnir safely recovered out of Jotunheim; and Freya the Beautiful came down to welcome them, smiling happily and leaning on the arm of Odur her husband.

7

THOR'S VISIT TO UTGARD

After Thor had recovered his hammer Miolnir,
killed Thrym the Giant with all his household,
and returned safely to Asgard without having to
give up Freya the Beautiful, the Giants begged
for peace with the Æsir. They even went so far as
to promise Thor and Loki safe conduct if they
would come on a visit to Utgard, the Giant city in
the heart of Jotunheim where Utgardhaloki was
king.

'No harm shall come to the Æsir, Thor
and Loki, or to any attendants they may bring,'
vowed Utgardhaloki, 'and I will send Skrymir my

messenger to lead them through Jotunheim. If he is not afraid, Thor will surely come.'

A challenge like this was the sure way of bringing Thor, and he ordered out his chariot forthwith and harnessed his two goats, Gaptooth and Cracktooth.

'They do not ask us out of friendship,' said cautious Loki. 'Some guile is intended, you may be certain.'

None the less he stepped into the chariot beside Thor, and off they drove in a great thundercloud across Midgard, the lightning flashing and flickering from the wheels as they went.

In the evening they came to a farmhouse on the edge of the river Ifing, the dark flood that never froze, which separated Midgard from Jotunheim. The good yeoman to whom it belonged welcomed his two strange guests, but confessed that he had very little food in the house, indeed scarcely enough for himself and his son and daughter, Thialfi and Roskva.

'That is no matter!' cried Thor, and killing his two goats Gaptooth and Cracktooth, he helped to flay and joint them. Very soon they were simmering in the pot, and the dinner was ready.

'Whatever you do,' Thor remarked, 'let none of the bones of my goats be broken.'

Then the meal began, and Thor showed his usual good appetite by eating one whole goat and a good deal of the other.

'What he said about the bones is only to keep

the marrow for himself,' whispered Loki the tempter to Thialfi, 'for it has strange and wonderful powers, since these are no ordinary goats.'

So Thialfi split one of the thigh bones when Thor was looking the other way, and scraped out some of the marrow with his knife. But he noticed that Loki was careful not to break any of the bones, so he contented himself with the one taste of marrow.

Thor and Loki slept that night in the farmhouse, and in the morning Thor flung all the bones into the goat-skins, waved Miolnir over them, and at once Gaptooth and Cracktooth sprang up as full of life as ever.

But one of them limped a little in his hind leg, and seeing this Thor turned with a roar of fury and whirled his hammer above his head to slay the yeoman and his two children.

'One of you has broken the thigh bone!' he shouted, his eyes flashing fire and his knuckles growing white as he gripped Miolnir.

The yeoman cowered on the floor, realizing who his terrible guest was, and promised any recompense he chose to ask.

Seeing the man's fear, Thor's brow cleared and he said:

'I will not smite. But your two children Thialfi and Roskva shall come with me, he to be my squire and she my handmaiden for ever more. See, it is an honour I do them and no evil . . . Now look well to my goats so that the bone is set and whole before our return. Roskva shall remain with you until then, but Thialfi comes with us now.'

So Thor and Loki continued their journey on foot, with Thialfi to attend on them. They went down beside the river Ifing until they reached the sea, and crossed where it was deepest in a boat that lay waiting for them. On the further shore they left the boat and advanced inland through a great forest. As evening approached they came out into open country among bare rocks and dark valleys; but nowhere could they find a house.

At last, just as darkness was beginning to fall, and they were feeling exceedingly tired and hungry, they came to a strange building. It was a great hall with an entrance so wide that it took up the whole end, but there was no one in it, no hearth nor fire, and no furniture.

It was better than nothing, however, in that freezing land, and the wayfarers made themselves as comfortable as possible in their strange lodging.

In the middle of the night they were wakened suddenly by a great earthquake, the ground shook all round them, and the hall trembled and swayed from side to side. Nothing else happened, but as he was exploring further Thor found a smaller room leading off the hall on the right-hand side, and into this his companions moved for greater warmth. Loki and the boy huddled together in the furthest corner, shaking with fear, but Thor gripped the handle of Miolnir firmly and stood on guard in the doorway. He could hear a roaring and a bellowing sound nearby, and from time to time a great crash: but he could see nothing.

At last the sky turned grey, and going out of the hall Thor saw in the first light of morning a Giant lying on the hillside a little distance away, snoring loudly. He was not a small Giant by any means – indeed he was the largest that Thor had ever seen.

Then Thor knew what the noises were that he had heard in the night, and in a fit of anger he girded himself with his belt of strength, and swung Miolnir in his hands, wondering where to strike.

At that moment the Giant woke, and Thor decided that it was safer not to use his hammer just then. Instead he asked:

'Who are you that have disturbed our slumbers with your snores?'

'I am Skrymir,' answered the Giant in a voice that echoed among the mountains. 'I have come to lead you to Utgard. I need not ask if you are Thor, for your hammer betrays you. But indeed you are rather smaller than I expected . . . Hallo, what have you been doing with my glove?'

With that he picked up what Thor had taken for a hall, shook Loki and Thialfi out of it, and put it on, slipping his thumb into the room where they had passed the night.

Then he opened his bag and made a huge breakfast: leaving Thor and his companions to be content with what they could find.

'I'll carry your bag of provisions in my own,' said Skrymir when he had finished his breakfast. 'Then we can dine together tonight in a more friendly fashion.'

Thor agreed readily, and Thialfi handed over the empty wallet, which Skrymir dropped into his own bag before lacing up the top and slinging it over his shoulder.

'Now follow me!' he boomed, and went striding away over the mountains while Thor and Loki did their best to keep up with him, and Thialfi followed painfully behind – though indeed he was the swiftest-footed of all men.

Late in the evening Skrymir found them shelter for the night under a mighty oak tree where they could get out of the bitter wind among its roots, and he lay on the hillside beyond its huge trunk.

'I am too tired to bother about supper,' said the Giant as he stretched himself out. 'But here is the food-bag: open it and help yourselves.'

He flung down his sack, and a few moments later was snoring like a volcano on the other side of the tree.

Thor set himself to unlace the food-bag; but pull and lever as he might, not a single thong could he loosen. Nor could he cut through the stiff leather.

'This Giant is mocking us!' he exclaimed at last, and in a rage he rushed round the tree and hit Skrymir on the head with Miolnir.

The Giant stirred in his sleep, yawned, and muttered sleepily:

'That was a big leaf which dropped on my head! . . . What are you doing, Thor? You have finished supper, I suppose, and are ready for bed?'

'We're just thinking about going to sleep,' growled Thor, and when Skrymir was snoring once more, he led Loki and Thialfi to another oak tree at a little distance where they settled down in hungry discomfort to get what rest they could.

Midnight came and Thor still could not sleep. Giant Skrymir had rolled on to his back and was snoring until the trees shook as if a great storm was raging.

'I'll silence that monster!' grumbled Thor. 'If we cannot eat, we might at least get a little sleep!'

He strode round to where Skrymir lay, planted his feet firmly, whirled Miolnir round his head and struck him on the crown with all his strength so that the hammer-head sank almost out of sight.

'What's happening now?' asked the Giant sitting up. 'Curse this oak tree! An acorn landed right on my head and woke me! . . . Or was it you, Thor, with news of some danger threatening us?'

'There's no danger that I know of,' answered Thor. 'It's now about midnight, and I had just woken and was stretching my legs for a few moments.'

Skrymir grunted, and went to sleep again; but Thor, bristling with fury, sat with hammer in hand planning how he would strike one more blow which should make an end of the Giant.

'If I can strike a really good one,' he thought to himself, 'he shall never see the light of day again!'

When dawn was just beginning to break Thor decided that his time had come. Skrymir appeared to be sleeping soundly, lying in such a way that Thor could reach one of his temples quite easily. So he rushed upon him whirling Miolnir with all his strength, and delivered a crashing blow.

Skrymir sat up suddenly and rubbed his head.

'It's those birds up in the oak tree!' he exclaimed. 'One of them dropped a twig on my forehead . . . Ah, Thor! So you're awake already. A good thing, for we have a long journey before us if you are to reach Utgard before night.'

They continued all day across the mountains, but as afternoon was advancing, Skrymir stopped and said to Thor:

'I must leave you here and go northwards. If you turn east you will reach Utgard before evening. But before we part, let me give you some advice. I heard you talking among yourselves and remarking that you had seen Giants smaller than I am. Let me warn you that in the castle of Utgard you will find several far taller than I. So when you get there be careful not to utter boastful words – for the followers of Utgardhaloki will not take them from such mere babes as you . . . In fact, my advice would be to turn back while you have the chance, and get home as quickly as you can.'

With that, Skrymir slung his bag over his shoulder and strode away towards the snow-covered mountains of the far north. And neither Thor nor Loki nor Thialfi was sorry to see him go.

They did not turn back, however, but went on towards the east, and as night was falling they came to a castle which was so high that it hurt the backs of their necks to look up to the top of it. There was an iron grating in the gateway, and this was closed. Thor strained his hardest to open it, but in vain: however they soon found that they were small enough to squeeze between the bars.

Inside they saw a mighty hall with wide-open doors, and on walking into it found many Giants sitting on benches along either side, while Utgard-haloki, the Giant King, sat at the high table on the dais at the end.

Thor and Loki saluted him politely, but at first he took no notice of them and went on picking his teeth. At length, however, he smiled at them scornfully, and said:

'As you seem to have come on a long journey, I suppose you are the Æsir from Asgard, and this small boy here must be Thor himself. Perhaps, however, you are greater than you seem: so tell us if you pride yourselves on any special accomplishments. We are all skilled here in feats of strength and endurance, and in craft and cunning as well. Now which of you will challenge one of us to prove his worth?'

'That I will!' cried Loki. 'There is one craft in which I excel, particularly at the moment, and that is eating. I'll have an eating match with any of you, and wager that no one can eat faster than I.'

'Well, that is a good contest,' said Utgardhaloki, 'and we will put you to the test at once. Our champion eater is called Logi, and he is ready to eat against you or anyone at any time.'

Then a great wooden trough was placed in the middle of the floor and filled with meat, and Loki sat down at one end and Logi at the other. Each set to work as fast as he could, and they met exactly in the middle.

'But Logi has won,' Utgardhaloki pointed out. 'For while Loki ate only the flesh, leaving the bare bones on the dish, Logi ate bones and dish and all!'

Presently Utgardhaloki looked at Thialfi and said: 'And this child? Is there anything he can do?'

'I'll run a race with any one of you who cares to try,' answered Thialfi boldly.

'A good accomplishment is running,' said Utgardhaloki, 'but you must be very swift if you are to outdistance my champion.'

Then he led the way out of the hall to a long strip of ground inside the castle walls. 'We will put you to the test at once,' he said, and called for Hugi, a young Giant, and bade him race with Thialfi.

The course was set and the two runners sped away. But in the first heat Hugi was so much ahead that when he reached the winning-post he turned round and went back to meet Thialfi.

Then said Utgardhaloki: 'You will need to exert yourself a bit more, Thialfi, if you are to beat Hugi – though no one who has come here has ever run faster than you have just done. Now try a second heat.'

They set off again, but this time Hugi reached the end of the course so long before Thialfi that he had time to turn and meet him a quarter of the way back.

'Thialfi has run this heat well also,' said Utgardhaloki, 'but I do not think that he can beat Hugi. However, he may have one more chance, and that shall decide the match.'

They set off for the third time, but now Hugi ran so fast that he was able to reach the winning-post, turn round, and meet Thialfi halfway back along the course.

'So Hugi is a better runner than Thialfi,' said Utgardhaloki as he led the way back into the hall. 'But these were only small contests. Thor, I am certain, will wish to show his strength, for we have heard great tales of his mighty deeds – and indeed we know that he has won victories against a Giant or two before now.'

'We came here in peace, and not to perform the deeds of war,' said Thor warily. 'But I am quite ready to contend with anyone in a drinking match.'

'An excellent notion,' cried Utgardhaloki, and

he bade one of his servants bring in the sconce-horn which was handed round among his warriors when they boasted of their powers of drinking.

'If one of us drinks this horn full at a single draught,' he said, 'we think well of him. Many a Giant, however, needs to pull at it twice; but we think very little of anyone who needs to raise it to his lips a third time.'

Thor took the horn, and it did not seem particularly big, except for its great length. He was very thirsty, and as he raised it to his lips he was confident that he would need to take no second draught to empty it. But when his breath failed and he raised his head from the horn and looked to see how much he had drunk, it seemed hardly any emptier than when he started.

'That was well drunk,' exclaimed Utgardhaloki, 'and yet it was not much. I would not have believed if I had not actually seen it that Thor of Asgard was so poor a drinker. Still, I feel sure you are only waiting to drain the horn at your next draught.'

Thor answered nothing, but raised the horn to his lips again, thinking that he would drink deeply indeed this time, and he strained at it until his breath gave out. Yet as he took the horn from his lips he realized that the end had not tilted up as far as it should; and when he came to look inside, it seemed as if less had gone than before: but now he could at least see below the rim.

'How now, Thor!' cried Utgardhaloki. 'You'll

drink again, surely, even if the third draught is more than is good for you? The third will surely be the greatest – but even if you empty the horn this time, you are not so mighty a champion as you are said to be among the Æsir. Though what you may yet do in other contests remains to be seen.'

At that Thor became angry. He raised the horn again and drank with all his might, straining until he could hold his breath no longer. He set down the horn and as he drew back gasping, he saw that at least the liquid in it had sunk quite a distance from the top. But he would not try again, and declared that he had drunk enough for one night.

'Now it is evident that you are not as mighty as we thought,' remarked Utgardhaloki. 'You cannot even swallow a little drink such as this. But will you try your hand at other games? You may do better in some feat of strength.'

'We hardly call such drinks as that little ones in Asgard,' grumbled Thor. 'But what game do you suggest now to try my strength?'

'Young lads here,' said Utgardhaloki, 'begin by a small trial of strength which is to lift my cat off the ground. I would not suggest so easy a test to Thor of the Æsir, did I not realize how very much less powerful you are than I expected.'

As he said this an enormous grey cat leapt into the middle of the floor and stood there spitting. Thor went forward and set his hands under its belly meaning to lift it by the middle. But the cat arched its back as Thor lifted, and though he strained upwards with all his strength he could only raise one paw off the ground.

'It is just as I expected,' smiled Utgardhaloki. 'But indeed my cat is a very large one, and our people are big and strong, not weak and puny like Thor the Thunderer.'

'Small as I am,' shouted Thor, 'I'll wrestle with any of you. For now you have angered me, my strength grows double!'

'I see no Giant here who would not think it a disgrace to wrestle with such a midget,' said Utgardhaloki looking round the hall. 'But we must not be deceived by appearances. Summon my old nurse, Elli, and let Thor wrestle with her. She has thrown men who seemed to me no less mighty than this great god of Asgard.'

Straightway there came into the hall an old woman, bent and stricken with years. Thor flushed angrily when he saw her, but Utgardhaloki insisted on the match, and when at last Thor took hold of her and tried to throw her, he discovered that it was not as easily done as he expected. In fact, the harder he gripped her the firmer she stood; and when she caught hold of him in her turn, Thor felt himself tottering on his feet, and in spite of all he could do she brought him to his knees.

'Enough of this!' cried Utgardhaloki. 'It is useless for Thor to try his strength with any of my warriors since he cannot even hold his own against this old woman. Sit down now, all three of you, and let us eat and drink. Only Loki has eaten and only Thor has drunk; but doubtless you can both take more of food and ale – for I would like you to see how well we in Utgard can entertain our guests.'

So they made good cheer far into the night, and slept there in the hall. And in the morning, when they were dressed and ready, Utgardhaloki drank a parting cup with them, and led them out of Utgard and well on their way back towards Midgard.

When he turned to bid them farewell he said: 'Now tell me, before we part, what you think of my castle of Utgard and the greatest of the Giant kind who live there? Do you admit that you have at last met Giants who are mightier than you?'

'I must confess,' said Thor sadly, 'that I have got little but shame from my dealings with you. When I am gone you will speak of me as a weakling, and I am ill content with that. It was with a very different purpose that I came to visit Utgard as the envoy of the Æsir.'

'Now I will tell you the truth,' said Utgardhaloki, 'since you are well away from my castle – which, if it is in my power, you shall never enter again. Indeed had I known how mighty you were, you had never come here at all: for so great is your strength that you have put us and all the world in deadly peril.

'Know then that I have cheated you with false seemings and illusions of the eye.

'To go back to the beginning: it was I who met you on the way, calling myself Skrymir; and as for my provision-bag, it was tied with iron made by Trolls – so that you could not possibly have untied it. Of the three blows you dealt me with your hammer Miolnir, the first was far the lightest, but it would have killed me if it had really landed on me. On your way home you will see a long mountain shaped like a saddle, with three deep gorges in it, one far deeper than the rest: those gorges you made with your hammer, for in each case I slipped aside so that the mountain received the blows and not I.

'In the same way I cheated you over your contests in my castle hall. The Giant against whom Loki ate so well was called Logi – and he was Fire itself which burned up the trough and bones as well as the meat. Thialfi ran against Hugi, who is Thought: and no man can run as swiftly as thought.

'When you drank from my horn, and the drink seemed to sink but slowly, you performed a wonder which I should not have believed possible. For the other end of the horn was joined to the sea, and it sank visibly throughout all the world when you drank. You caused the first ebb-tide: and the tides shall ebb and flow for ever more in memory of your deed.

'When you strove to lift my cat we were all in deadly terror. For he was the Midgard Serpent which stretches round the whole world – and when you raised it, the head and tail of Jormungand scarcely touched the ground.

'Finally, your last feat was as remarkable as the rest. For Elli with whom you wrestled was Old Age – and yet she only brought you to your knees, though never a man lived, nor shall ever live, who will not at the last be vanquished by Old Age.

'Now we must part, and it will be best for both of us if you never come here to seek me again. Should you do so, I will defend my castle by wiles such as I have already used against you – or by others. But if you stay away from Jotunheim, there may be peace between the Æsir and the Giants.'

Then a sudden gust of fury filled Thor, and he whirled up Miolnir to fling at Utgardhaloki, deeming that this time there should be no mistake.

But Utgardhaloki was gone; and suddenly the mist came down from the mountains so that when Thor turned back to destroy the castle of Utgard and crush it to pieces, there was no castle to be seen.

So Thor, Loki, and Thialfi turned and groped their way through the fog, back into the mountains, and they could scarcely see more than a few yards in front of them until they came to the great mountain with the three gorges which Thor had cleft with his hammer.

Beyond it the fog cleared, and they made their way easily enough until they came to the farmhouse where Thor had left his chariot.

The goat whose bone had been broken by Thialfi had now quite recovered, and next day they set out for Asgard, taking Roskva with them.

When Thor told Odin and the other Æsir how Utgardhaloki had tricked him, and repeated what he had told him before they parted, Odin said:

'You have done well in the Land of the Giants, though at first it seemed but ill. For now they know our strength – and we know what they can do to outwit us. We may not be able to destroy them, but I do not think that they will come against Asgard, nor overrun Midgard. Yet they will come against us at Ragnarok, on the Day of the Last Great Battle.'

'Nevertheless I am determined to wipe out this insult to my prowess in Giant blood,' growled Thor.

'You need not doubt that Giant blood will still be shed,' answered Odin. 'Though we are at peace with Utgardhaloki, there are Giants who will still try to harm us or to bring ruin to men in Midgard. I do not think the hammer Miolnir will ever grow rusty!'

'No!' muttered Thor. 'And when I have conquered the Giants, I am determined to try my strength against the Midgard Serpent! Had I known that Utgardhaloki's cat was Jormungand, instead of trying to lift its paw from the ground I would have stroked its head with Miolnir!'

8

ODIN GOES WANDERING

There was peace throughout the Nine Worlds:
the Dwarfs were busy at their forges under the
earth; in Jotunheim the Giants rested uneasily
after Thor's visit, and plotted no new evil against
Asgard. In Muspelheim, the fire region, all was
quiet, waiting for the Day of Ragnarok. Elves and
Vanir dwelt in happiness; in Hela's hard land
and in misty Nifelheim nothing stirred. Odin and
Frigga his queen rose up in Asgard and took their
way across Bifrost Bridge to visit Midgard, to
wander disguised in the world of men.

Now it chanced that good King Raudung had

two young sons named Gerrad and Agnar, and one day the boys set out in a small boat to fish in the smooth sea near their father's kingdom.

Suddenly the clouds banked up over the clear sky and a great storm rose with a mighty wind which carried the little boat far away from the land. The boys clung to the sides expecting every moment to be overset and drowned; but at last they came to a little island where the boat ran aground and they struggled on to dry land more dead than alive.

Night was coming on, and they saw a glow of light in the distance. Towards this they crawled, and found a little cottage with smoke coming from the chimney and firelight flickering behind the windows.

Agnar knocked at the door, and it was opened by an old, one-eyed man in a broad-brimmed hat. He welcomed the two boys into the cottage, and he and his wife warmed them by the fire, fed them, and made them comfortable for the night.

Winter was coming on before the boys were fully recovered from their shipwreck, and the two old peasants kept them until the spring, treating them as if they were their own children.

During the long months on the island the boys learnt many things from their kind foster-parents. Their host taught them the use of the bow and the spear, to wrestle and to run, to wield the sword and to swing both axe and hammer. But sometimes his wife led them away into the woods and taught them about all living things, from the song of the birds to the use of herbs to cure sickness or heal wounds.

And in the long nights of winter they told the two boys about the doings of gods and men, the glories of battle and the greater glories of honour and hospitality.

Spring came at last, and when the sun of early summer smiled upon the sea, Gerrad and Agnar launched their boat again and made ready to set sail.

Then the two old peasants came down to the seashore and blessed the two children.

'Hoist this sail,' said the woman, and her voice sounded suddenly young and strong, the voice of a great queen. 'And I will send a strong, sweet breeze to waft you across the waves to your home in safety.'

'Go, my children,' said the man, and he too seemed younger, and he drew himself up as if he were a great king sending out his warriors to battle. 'You came to us as children, but you go from us as young men, tall and strong, on the very threshold of your lives. Live worthily, and come at the last to the glad halls of Valhalla.'

As the boat skimmed away over the waters, Agnar and Gerrad turned and saw the stately figures of Odin and Frigga standing on the shore behind them.

All that day Gerrad and Agnar sailed over the dancing waves, and in the evening they came to the land where their father King Raudung ruled. Agnar rejoiced at the thought of their homecoming, and was about to spring on to the land as the boat touched the shore in the twilight, when Gerrad turned upon him suddenly:

'Sail away, Agnar!' he cried. 'Go to the land where Giants and Trolls may seize you!'

With that he struck him so that he fell back senseless into the boat, and Gerrad pushed it back into the sea. The out-going tide caught it and the currents whirled it away into the distance.

Gerrad then went up to his father's palace and was welcomed eagerly by the old king.

'But where is Agnar your brother?' he asked.

'Alas,' said Gerrad, 'he was lost at sea on our perilous voyage. A great wave swept him into the water, and do what I might, I could not save him.'

Very soon after this Raudung died, and Gerrad became king in his place, and grew famous for his wealth and feared by his foes.

But Agnar drifted away until the boat brought him to the Land of the Giants. There he was kindly treated, for indeed his goodness and gentleness made even the Giants forget their cruel ways.

In time, however, he began to long for his home; and at last he set out in disguise and came to the hall of King Gerrad his brother. Here he did not reveal himself, but became a servant in his own home, serving the cruel, miserly king, and helping all those whom he could.

Meanwhile Odin and Frigga had returned to Asgard, and one day as they sat together in Lidskialf looking out over the world, Odin said:

'Did you see our foster-son Agnar whom you loved? Of late he dwelt among the Giants our enemies, and I believe that he was even married to a Giantess. How much better has his brother Gerrad turned out to be: see him, a mighty king ruling his father's land well and wisely.'

But Frigga replied: 'Gerrad is cruel and miserly. He strove to kill Agnar his brother, and he is sparing of his food even to the guests within his doors.'

'I will visit him in disguise,' said Odin, 'and prove whether your words are just. I am about to go down into Midgard on my way to Jotunheim to have speech with Valfthrudnir the wise Giant, for he boasts that he knows more of the secrets of the universe than I do myself. I would learn if he has indeed anything to teach me: but if it is all idle boasting, I shall punish him as he deserves.'

'I counsel you, father of gods and men, to stay here in Asgard,' answered Frigga. 'Valfthrudnir is indeed the wisest of the Giants: but he is our enemy, and his wisdom may be but a trap to draw you into Jotunheim to your peril.'

But Odin replied: 'Far have I travelled, much have I seen and many beings have I known. Yet never did I hold converse with a wise Giant such as Valfthrudnir, and him I must visit.'

'May all go well with you, then,' said Frigga

anxiously. 'Both on your journey there, and on your way back to Asgard. And may your wisdom stand you in good stead when you come to bandy words with this Giant.'

So Odin wrapped himself in a long blue cloak, drew his broad-brimmed hat well over his brows, and set off through Midgard, giving out that he was a wise man named Grimnir who knew many Runes of power, and was learned in what the Norns decreed for the future, as well as in knowledge of the past.

He came at last to the land where Gerrad ruled, and begged a night's lodging at the palace.

Now while Odin was on his way, Frigga had sent her handmaiden Fulla to King Gerrad with a message:

'Have a care of the man in the blue cloak. He is more than he seems, and you may know this since no dog, however savage, will so much as bark at him.'

In his evil heart Gerrad took this to mean only one thing: that the man in the blue cloak must be a wicked sorcerer, coming to his land to cast evil spells upon him and his people.

He therefore let loose his fiercest dogs, and bade his men be ready to seize the stranger when he arrived.

Sure enough, one night an old man in a blue cloak and wide-brimmed hat came walking up to the gate before the palace. Then the fierce dogs ran out to attack him: but as they drew near, one

and all put their tails between their legs, and
slunk away without a sound.

When Gerrad saw that the dogs did not even
bark at the stranger, he told his men to seize him
at once.

'Who are you?' he demanded, 'and what are
you doing here?'

'I am a poor traveller called Grimnir,' was the
answer, 'and I am on a journey about my own
business. But when you have given me the welcome due from so great a king to the poor stranger
at his hearth, I will tell you things from my
wisdom which it were well for you to know.'

'Oh, I'll warm you at my hearth, never fear,'
answered Gerrad grimly, 'and you'll tell me all
you know very soon!'

Then he ordered his men to tie Grimnir between two fires, and make sure to keep them well
stoked and burning fiercely until the wicked sorcerer should confess why he had dared to come
there.

For eight days and nights Grimnir sat between
the fires with neither food nor drink, suffering
cruelly. On the eighth night the servant, who was
Agnar in disguise, crept quietly to the captive
between the fires and gave him a great horn filled
with refreshing mead.

Grimnir drained it to the last drop, and said in
a low voice:

'All hail to you, Agnar the Good. The chief of
the Æsir, father of gods and men, wishes you

well. Never for one draught of mead shall you receive a richer reward.'

Agnar drew back in fear and wonder, and as he did so the prisoner between the two fires – which were already scorching his own skin – flung back his head and began to sing in a clear deep voice.

He sang of the high halls of Asgard: of how in the beginning Odin built great halls for the Æsir; of Thrudheim the strong dwelling of Thor, and fair Yewdales where Uller lived; of Alfheim over which Frey was lord and of Valhalla where day by day Odin chose his Heroes from men killed in battle; of Thrymheim where Giant Thiassi lived until the Æsir slew him and set his eyes among the stars; of Breidablik where sun-bright Baldur had his hall, the most blessed of dwellings, and of Heavenhold where Heimdall the keen-eyed watch-man of the Æsir drank his mead in peace; of Folkvanger where beauteous Freya welcomed those whom she chose from among the battle-slain; of Glitnir the Shining House where Forseti the wise son of Baldur sat in judgement every day; and of quiet Noatun by the sounding sea where Niord lived.

He sang of the Ash Yggdrasill the great World Tree, and its three roots; of Nid Hog who gnawed at the lowest, and of Ratatosk the squirrel who scampered among the branches. Also he sang of the mysteries of Day and Night, of the chariots of Moon and Sun and of the wolves that chase them through the sky.

As he sang Gerrad drew near to him, and his face was dark with fury. But the rage turned to fear as the song drew to its close and Grimnir rose slowly to his feet, the bonds falling from his wrists and his one eye flashing.

'Ah, Gerrad!' he cried. 'Too deeply have you drunk of the mead of evil. Grievous is it for you who were so favoured to have lost and forfeited the friendship of Odin and the place kept for you in his hall of the chosen . . . The friends that *you* have chosen cannot help you. I see your sword already dripping with your blood: your life is at an end and the Norns cut the thread of it. Now you see Odin face to face, for I am he! . . . Gerrad, come to me if you can!'

Gerrad sprang forward to kneel and beg Odin's forgiveness, but as he did so, his sword slipped from its sheath, he stumbled, tried to catch it and fell forward so that it pierced him to the heart and he lay dead.

Odin turned to the poorly clad servant who had brought him the horn of mead:

'Come forth, Agnar the Good!' he cried. 'Raudung's son and Gerrad's brother shall now reign in this land. May the blessing of Odin rest upon it, for I know that you will rule well and justly, showing mercy to all and kindness to strangers most of all.'

Then, leaving Agnar to his long and glorious reign over his people the Goths, Odin gathered his cloak about him, put on his broad-brimmed hat, and went out into the night on his way to Jotunheim.

He came in time to the hall of Valfthrudnir the Giant and asked for shelter.

'My name is Gangradur,' he said, 'and I come from far away. In my own land I am counted the wisest of those who dwell there, and I would compete with you in knowledge of high things, both past and to come.'

'Why do you stand in the doorway?' cried Valfthrudnir. 'Come into the hall and be seated. I make you welcome, for you shall never leave my hall unless you go forth as victor: for know that he who fails in this test of wisdom loses his head.'

'That I know well,' answered the guest who called himself Gangradur. 'Now begin your questions, if, knowing the penalty, you dare to compete with an unknown stranger who does not choose to say from whence he comes.'

'If you were Odin himself,' cried Valfthrudnir with a cruel laugh, 'I would still have your head. For not even the chief of the Æsir knows more than I.'

The Giant then began to ask such questions as those which had passed between Odin and Alviss the Dwarf – the names of the horses of Day and Night, of the river that severs Asgard from Jotunheim, and of the Field where Ragnarok is to be fought.

'Shinfaxi, the horse Sheen-mane draws the Day chariot,' answered Gangradur, 'and Rimfaxi, the horse Rime-mane takes Night on her way. Ifing is the river, dark and unfreezing, that severs the Æsir from the Giants, and on Vigrid Plains shall the Last Battle be fought.'

Then it was the stranger's turn to ask questions, and his were of the making of earth and heaven, of Ginnungagap and the Giant Ymir, of how Niord of the Vanir came to Asgard, concerning the Norns and their wisdom, and of who should live after the Twilight of the Gods.

'Wise are you indeed,' said Gangradur, 'but can you tell me what shall be the fate of Odin in the Last Great Battle, on the day of Ragnarok?'

'The Wolf shall devour him,' answered Valfthrudnir, 'and Vidar shall avenge him, rending apart the jaws that slay.'

'Far have I travelled,' said Gangradur, 'and untold things have I tried; into worlds unknown have I been and questioned many creatures. Therefore tell me – and if you know it, I indeed grant you the wisest of Giants – tell me what word of hope shall Odin whisper into the dead ear of his son as he lies upon the funeral pyre.'

Then the Giant Valfthrudnir knew that it was Odin himself who questioned him, and he bowed his head for the sword-blow, saying:

'No being knows what word you spoke in your dead son's ear, long ago in the web of the Norns yet long ages on in the future. With a doomed mouth have I bandied questions of the world's doom, for you are Odin – and you shall ever be the wisest of all.'

'Your head is forfeit to me,' said Odin gravely, 'but I will not take it now. Only have a care lest you boast again of your wisdom or by any means harm such guests as come to seek your hospitality.'

Odin went on his way once more, but when he was gone into the night he cast from him his disguise, and stood forth in his own form, king of the Æsir and lord of mankind, a noble figure with flashing sword and golden helm.

And, as if in answer to his very thought, the great horse Sleipnir came to him, the horse of Odin with its eight legs and flowing mane. He leapt upon its back and went forward through Jotunheim: but he had not crossed the dark river Ifing by the time the sun rose, and it chanced that he passed by the dwelling of Rungnir, the great Giant of the Mountains.

As he drew near, Rungnir himself rode out to meet him, and accosted him in friendly fashion:

'What manner of man are you?' he shouted. 'Never before did I see such a warrior, with a golden helmet on his head riding upon an eight-legged steed, and passing at will through air and water.'

'I am of the Æsir who dwell in Asgard,' answered Odin, 'and there is no such steed as mine in all the Nine Worlds. I'll wager my head that you have none in Jotunheim that can go so fast or so far.'

'Your head against mine!' cried Rungnir. 'My

horse Golden Mane is a better mount than yours.
There is no doubt of it: you have lost your head already.'

'Catch and pass me, if so you think!' cried
Odin, and setting spurs to Sleipnir he was on the
next hill-top in a moment.

But now a Giant's frenzy seized upon Rungnir.
He spurred Golden Mane and followed Odin swift
as the storm wind or the avalanche down the
mountain-side.

Odin rode fast and far, speeding through the
clouds, while Sleipnir spurned the mountain tops
with his hooves. He came first to Asgard, and
turned to meet Rungnir in the entrance way.

The Giant leapt from foaming Golden Mane
and stood in the Gate of the Æsir.

'Come in as a guest and drink with us,' said
Odin, 'for you have a right good steed – and yet
your head is mine if I cared to claim it.'

So Rungnir strode into the hall and cried aloud
for the biggest horn of mead in all Valhalla. Thor
was not present, so his horn was brought to the
Giant, and those flagons in which his drink was
stored.

Rungnir drained the horn, and then swilled
down the mead from one flagon after another,
until he became drunk and began to boast and
shout threats.

'This is a fair hall!' he cried. 'I'll carry it away
with me! Jotunheim shall be the home of Valhalla,
not Asgard . . . You'll try to stop me? I don't fear

the Æsir – I'll kill them all! . . . No, I won't kill lovely Freya and golden-haired Sif: I'll take them home with me . . . Come, pour me more mead . . . What, do none of you dare?'

Freya alone had the courage to pour mead into his horn, and Rungnir drank deeply once more, shouting:

'I'll drink all the ale of the Æsir! Not a drop shall there be left in Asgard. Then I'll go back to my home in Jotunheim, with Freya and Sif to be my bond-women! Who dares stop me?'

At this moment Thor strode into the hall, swinging his hammer Miolnir in his hand, and his eyes flashed fire when he saw the drunken Giant sitting there.

'Who has allowed a foul Giant to set foot in Asgard?' he shouted. 'Who has given Rungnir safe conduct into Valhalla? How comes it that lovely Freya is pouring mead for one of our enemies from Jotunheim?'

'I come as a guest,' growled Rungnir, glaring at Thor. 'Odin himself invited me to drink mead with the Æsir in Valhalla.'

'You shall repent accepting that invitation before you get away from here!' thundered Thor.

'Little renown will you gain, great Thor, if you kill me now, unarmed as I am,' cried Rungnir. 'But if you want to show your courage, meet me in single combat on the borders of Jotunheim, at Giottunagard, the Place of Rolling Stones.'

'Get you back to Jotunheim and arm yourself,'

roared Thor. 'Then meet me at Giottunagard with but one squire to support you, whoever you may choose. I will be there to meet you, and we fight to the death.'

Then Rungnir leapt upon Golden Mane and galloped furiously until he came to Jotunheim. There he told the Giants of what had chanced, and of the great battle which was to be.

'You must win,' said the Giants. 'If Thor is victorious he will invade Jotunheim in his pride – for you are the strongest of all Giants, and Thor bears us a grudge since Utgardhaloki tricked him and Loki when they visited Utgard.'

So the Giants went to Giottunagard and there they made a man out of clay to be Rungnir's squire. This clay Giant was nine miles high and three miles broad across the chest. Their greatest difficulty was to find a heart large enough for him: for that they could not make. Finally they took a mare's heart, as that was the largest they could find, and set it in his breast of clay.

Rungnir's own heart was of stone, three-pronged and sharp like the Runic letter 'Y', which is called Rungnir's Heart for this reason. His head also was of stone, so that his brain was none of the best, and he had a stone shield as well.

When the day of battle arrived the combatants set out for Giottunagard. The clay man was the first to see Thor approaching: and at the sight his knees knocked together and he grew damp all over.

But Thialfi the fleet-footed squire dashed up to Rungnir and cried:

'Giant, I give you a word of warning! You will lose the battle if you hold your shield in front of you! For Thor has seen you, and has gone underground. He's coming against you from underneath – up through the earth!'

When Rungnir heard this, he placed his stone shield on the ground and stood on it, which left him free so that he could grip his weapon, which was a hone cut from a great mass of whetstone, with both hands.

Scarcely was he ready when he saw Thor coming against him in a blaze of lightning, with the thunder rumbling under his footsteps. Roaring with rage, Thor whirled up his great hammer Miolnir and flung it at Rungnir. The Giant lifted his hone and cast it at Thor at the same moment, and the two weapons crashed together in mid air. The hone broke into pieces, scattering over the earth to form all the veins of whetstone and flint rock: but one piece hit Thor on the forehead so that he fell to the ground on his face.

But Miolnir struck Rungnir on the head and shattered his stone skull to tiny crumbs no bigger than grains of sand, so that he fell dead with one foot across Thor's neck.

Meanwhile Thialfi the nimble had attacked the clay man with a spade, and as the clay of which he was made was already wet and soft he was able to break him up in a few minutes and spread him like marl over the fields.

Then he turned to help Thor who was still pinned to the earth by Rungnir's foot. But try though he might he could not raise the Giant's limb.

By this time the Æsir, hearing of Thor's mishap, had arrived at Giottunagard; and they also tried to raise Rungnir's foot. But not even great Odin himself, nor strong Tyr, nor Uller of the mighty arms, nor Loki the cunning, could set Thor free.

But Thor's own son Magni, who was then but three years old, came to see what had happened to his father; and when he saw the Giant's foot resting on Thor's neck, he raised it easily and flung it aside.

'What a pity it is that I came so late,' he exclaimed. 'If I'd been here sooner I would have killed this Giant with a blow of my fist, and saved you all this trouble.'

'You are like to be as mighty a Giant-killer as I am, when you are fully grown,' said Thor proudly as he rose to his feet. 'Now, in memory of this your first feat of strength, I will give you the horse Golden Mane which belonged to this dead Giant.'

'The horse should have been mine,' said Odin gravely. 'But I do not grudge it to my valiant grandson – though his mother is a Giantess.' For Magni's mother was not Sif the golden-haired, but Jarnsaxa of the Iron Knife, the strongest of all the Giantesses in Jotunheim.

So the Æsir returned victorious to Asgard, after making peace with the Giants, who were thoroughly frightened by the death of Rungnir and the destruction of the clay monster.

At home in Thrudvangar his massive hall Thor sat still in moody discomfort, holding his aching head. For the splinter of stone which had struck him was still fixed in his skull, and neither he nor Magni could pull it out or stop the pain it caused him.

In vain Sif bathed the wound with her gentle fingers, and wept over it with her dew-like tears.

'Rungnir's hone must have been cut and shaped by magic,' growled Thor at last. 'Doubtless some Rune of enchantment is graven on the piece of whetstone in my head, and only by sorcery can it be removed.'

So they sent for Groa the Witch, the wife of Aurvandill the Brave, who of all men in Midgard was most feared by the Giants and who would go alone into Jotunheim and there slay them by trickery.

Groa came willingly to Thrudvangar, for Thor had come to Aurvandill's aid more than once on his expeditions into Jotunheim. Now she drew magic Runes on the floor and began to sing strange, mysterious songs and chant spells as she held her hands above his head.

Thor felt the splinter of stone working loose, and the pain faded from him. Anxious, in his relief and gratitude, to repay Groa for her help, he said:

'I have news for you which will make you glad. When last I wandered in Jotunheim I found Aurvandill your husband in sore danger from the Giants. But I was able to rescue him and carry him away to safety. I hid him in a basket on my back when I waded through Elivagar the Ice Brook. And I'll give you a proof of how highly we of Asgard value your husband in his war on the Giants. As we crossed that river of bitter cold I saw that one of his toes was sticking out of the basket and had become frozen solid. So I broke it off and tossed it up into the sky where it has turned into the brightest of all the stars. But Aurvandill is alive and well, and is on his way home to you.'

When Groa heard this, she was so excited that she forgot about her charms and incantations. Instead she turned and hurried out of Thrudvangar as fast as she could in her eagerness to be at home in time to welcome her husband Aurvandill on his return.

So the splinter of whetstone remained in Thor's head, though the pain of it was cured. But ever afterwards it was forbidden in Midgard to fling a hone across the floor, or even to drop it on the ground: for whenever that was done, the stone stirred in Thor's forehead and caused his head to ache.

9

GEIRRODUR THE TROLL KING

Thor rested in Thrudvangar after his battle with Rungnir, and the Giants were left in peace. And indeed the truce between Asgard and Jotunheim still held, whatever battle there might be between an occasional Giant and one of the Æsir.

But Loki, ever in search of mischief, set out in his favourite disguise as a falcon to spy in Midgard and Jotunheim and to stir up what trouble he could. For Loki's mischief grew more spiteful the more he indulged in it, and his evil Giant-nature was slowly triumphing over his blood-brotherhood with the Æsir.

On this occasion, after dawdling through Midgard and leading men astray, Loki came to the Vimur, widest of all rivers, which separated Midgard from that province of Jotunheim where the Stone Trolls and the Fire Trolls had their dwellings.

The Trolls were strange, misshapen creatures related to both the Giants and the Dwarfs. Their homes were under low hills which they could raise on red pillars to let in an occasional glimmer of light; they were smiths like the Dwarfs, and hoarded great treasures, but they had little of the Dwarfs' skill. They lived wild, savage lives, delighting in dirt and evil smells, and they were often servants of the Giants and usually in league with them against the Æsir and the Men of Midgard.

In the land beyond the Vimur the Giant Geirrodur was king, and his castle was a Troll house larger than any of the rest, a great mountain with a chimney in the centre that belched out black smoke which would sweep down over all the country like an evil fog.

Loki was interested in the Trolls, and most curious to see what they were at in Geirrodur's huge castle. So he perched on the sill of a window high up in the outer wall, and looked down into the hall where the Giant and his two daughters, Gialp and Greip, were sitting at dinner in golden chairs set on a floor that was thick with filth.

Geirrodur looked up and saw Loki at the window and called to his Troll servants:

'Fetch me that bird which is perching up there. I have often longed for a falcon such as the Æsir and the thanes and kings of Midgard carry on their wrists.'

Loki was not in the least frightened, and as the Trolls came clambering awkwardly up the rough stone wall he decided to give them as much trouble and danger as possible before he flew away.

As the first Troll drew near the window, Loki hopped up the side of it, and kept just out of reach, holding on to the stones of the wall with his claws. Backwards and forwards over the castle wall he went, always getting a little bit higher. The Trolls climbed after him, cursing and grunting as again and again the bird slipped out of their hands just as one of them was about to clutch him.

At last Loki came to the top of the wall, and as one of the Trolls was very near him, he decided he had had enough of this sport, and spread his wings to fly away.

But to his horror the wall held his feet like a magnet, and he could not escape. Then a Troll's hand closed on him and he was carried down in triumph to Geirrodur.

The Giant took the falcon in his great hands and looked at it carefully.

'This is no bird,' he exclaimed at last. 'It is some man, or one of the Æsir, disguised as a bird. His eyes betray him, for they cannot be changed as the body can. So speak, bird, and tell me who you are and why you come fluttering about my castle – speak, or it will be the worse for you.'

Loki said nothing, however, and did his best to pretend that he was in truth only a bird. But Geirrodur was not to be deceived, and when he found that his captive would not speak he shut him up securely in a great stone chest.

'There you shall stay, without food or drink, air or light, until you speak!' he cried as he slammed down the lid.

And there Loki remained for three months, until he could bear it no longer, and at last he called out to Geirrodur:

'I am Loki, one of the greatest of the Æsir. I did not come here to harm you. Indeed you may have heard of me: after Odin I have no equal among the Æsir except Thor the enemy of the Giants ... And Thor I do not love, for I myself am of the Giant kin.'

'I have no love for Thor either,' growled Geirrodur, 'nor for any of the Æsir. And I'll wring your neck here and now and throw you back into that chest and seal it up for ever under a mountain – unless you can bring Thor here to my castle. But he must come without his hammer: against Miolnir no Giant can stand, not even I!'

Then Loki swore the most solemn oaths that he would do so, or return and give himself up to Geirrodur; and the Giant let him go, for he knew that even Loki would not break the oath of the Æsir – or else Asgard would be closed to him for ever.

Loki flew away from Geirrodur's castle, back across the wide Vimur and over Midgard until he came near the foot of Bifrost Bridge. There he took on his own shape again, and came up into Asgard, letting Heimdall the Watchman think that he had been wandering among men to help and instruct them.

In Asgard he let fall a remark or two about the friendly Giant Geirrodur in his wonderful castle built by the clever Trolls.

'He entertained me very kindly,' said Loki, sipping his mead thoughtfully in Valhalla. 'He showed me wonderful things which I have seen nowhere else . . . He said how much he would like to entertain great Thor and give him gifts from his treasury: but he does not dare to ask, for he is afraid of the mere sight of the hammer Miolnir which has slain so many of the Giants.'

Loki talked like this whenever Thor was listening, and at last his tempting words took effect, for the Thunderer still always slow to suspect evil, even of a Giant – and he was did not realize how ready Loki had become to betray the Æsir and help the Giants to overcome them, simply to satisfy his private grudges and his evil spite.

So Thor set out one day with his squire Thialfi, leaving Miolnir hanging in Thrudvangar. Over Midgard they drove in the goat-drawn chariot, the thunder rumbling behind them, and came at last to the shores of Vimur, to the great house where Grid lived.

She was a friendly Giantess who had helped Odin in the early days of the world, and she was the mother of his son Vidar the Silent, the Lord of the Forests.

Grid entertained Thor kindly, for she loved all the Æsir, and as they sat at dinner she asked him where he was going so near the edge of Jotunheim without Miolnir in his hand.

'I am going to visit Geirrodur the Troll King,' answered Thor. 'For he is the friend of the Æsir and has bidden me as his guest to visit his castle and feast there with him. I hear that he has treasures such as even we of Asgard have never seen. Loki the cunning passed many days with him, and he was lost in wonder at what he has seen in Geirrodur's castle.'

'I fear that Loki the cunning has been playing you false,' said Grid. 'For I know well that Geirrodur the Troll King is an evil and a crafty Giant, very ill to deal with, and no friend to any of the Æsir – least of all to him from whose hand Miolnir has sped so often to be the death of Giants.'

'I am glad of this warning,' answered Thor, 'but I cannot now turn back, or the Giants would think me a coward.'

'Go forward then to Geirrodur's castle,' said Grid, 'but take with you my Girdle of Might, and this iron staff which is called Grid's Rod, and these iron gloves. With them you may hold your own against Geirrodur and his Trolls. Be very wary of his craft and treachery, for I do not know how he is planning to bring doom upon you.'

Next day, leaving his chariot with Grid, Thor set out on foot followed only by Thialfi, and went up beside the Vimur river until it grew narrower as it came rushing out of the deep valleys among the mountains of Jotunheim.

Here Thor fastened the Girdle of Might round his waist and stepped into the swirling water, steadying himself with Grid's Rod against the rush of the current. And Thialfi followed behind him, clinging on to the Girdle of Might so as not to be swept away.

When Thor reached the middle of the river it seemed to him that the current grew suddenly twice as strong, and the water began to rise round his chest and surge over his shoulders.

As the water still rose and the flood poured down faster than ever, Thor looked upstream and saw Geirrodur's giant daughter Gialp standing with a foot on either bank where the river raced through a mighty chasm in the rocks; and he saw that she was making the flood.

'A river should be dammed at its source!' he cried, and stooping down he snatched up a great rock from the river and flung it at her with such good aim that the flood was stopped and he was able to reach the other side.

Here the current lifted him off his feet, but he was able to catch at a mountain ash which grew out from the bank. Holding on to this he drew Thialfi and himself to safety: and for this reason the ash was ever afterwards called Thor's Tree of Deliverance.

Once safely on the further bank of the Vimur river, Thor and Thialfi made their way easily until they came in sight of Geirrodur's huge mountain-castle, where the black smoke was pouring in clouds out of the great chimney in the centre.

As they drew near Trolls met them and made them welcome in the name of their King.

'Come with us to the guest house,' they said. 'A room is prepared for you, and there you must wait for a little while until Geirrodur is ready to receive you worthily in his great hall.'

They were shown into a big stone-roofed room next to the hall, and there the Trolls left them alone for a little.

Thor, who was tired after his struggle in the river, sat down thankfully in the only chair and leant back to rest. But suddenly he felt the chair rising from the floor and moving up towards the roof to crush him against the stone beams.

Quick as lightning Thor thrust Grid's Rod against the roof and pushed back with all his might, forcing the chair down towards the floor again. Then he heard a great crack, a crash, and screams coming from beneath him.

He sprang up, and there under the chair were Geirrodur's two daughters, Gialp and Greip, with their backs broken.

Thor tightened the Girdle of Might, pulled on the iron gloves, and strode out of the guest house in a fury.

'Geirrodur's daughters are rightly punished!' he exclaimed. 'They tried to crush me against the roof. Now I must see if Geirrodur himself is so wicked that he plots to kill the guest in his very hall.'

Outside the guest house the Trolls were waiting, and they led Thor and Thialfi into the great hall. Here many big fires were burning on either side, and through the smoke and flames Thor could see Geirrodur the Giant standing at the further end beside the hottest fire of all.

Thor advanced slowly up the hall, and when he drew near to the Troll King, Geirrodur suddenly drew a bar of white-hot metal out of the fire with a huge pair of tongs and flung it at him.

But Thor was walking warily. And when he saw the bar of white-hot metal hurtling towards him he caught it with his iron gloves, whirled it round his head, and hurled it back at Geirrodur.

The Troll King saw it coming and dodged behind an iron pillar to save himself. But the bar passed right through the pillar, through Geirrodur standing behind it, through the wall of the castle, and deep into the earth beyond that.

Then Thor turned and strode out of the hall, whirling Grid's Rod in his hands and smiting down Trolls on either side. Without so much as a backward glance, he and Thialfi walked down to the ford over the river Vimur, crossed it easily this time, and made their way back to Grid's dwelling.

There Thor gave her back the Rod and the gloves, but by her wish he kept the Girdle of Might, and with this about his waist he mounted his chariot and drove triumphantly back to Asgard.

Thor did not trouble himself further about Geirrodur and the Troll Castle, he did not even deign to tell Loki of what had chanced there. Nevertheless the fame of it, and of what he had done on that visit, spread through Midgard, and at last a king of Denmark named Gorm decided to set out in search of Geirrodur's Castle.

He took with him three ships and the wise traveller Thorkill, and set sail over the sea towards the great river Vimur, which to the men of Midgard seemed as wide as the ocean itself.

Over the sea they sailed for many days, the wind blowing softly, so that they moved but slowly; and when at last they came to land, there was little food left in the ships and all the men were hungry.

On shore they found great herds of cattle wandering about, so tame that they would let a man walk right up to them.

'Kill only what we need for one day's food,' Thorkill warned them. 'If you kill more, the powers who rule this island will seek revenge.'

But the men paid no attention to his advice and slaughtered many of the cattle to take with them for future use. In the night an army of Trolls attacked them, and a Giant who was their leader came wading through the sea waving a huge club and threatening to destroy the ships and everyone in them if they did not give up one man from each ship as a fine for slaughtering the cattle.

It seemed better to do this than to let all perish, so three men were chosen by lot and handed over to the Trolls, and the ships sailed on their way.

They came at length to a land of deep snow and frozen peaks, where monsters lurked in the dark forests; and here they landed, Thorkill telling them that nearby was the castle of Geirrodur.

'But have a care,' Thorkill advised the King and his companions. 'Those who dwell here will seek to work us evil. Therefore speak to no one; but let me, who know the ways of this place and all its dangers, do such talking as is needed.'

As twilight approached a Giant came striding down to the beach, much to the terror of King Gorm and his followers.

But Thorkill reassured them. 'This is Gudmund, the brother of Geirrodur,' he told them. 'He will have come to offer us hospitality. But have a care: take with you any food that you need, and touch nothing that is offered you and touch none of the people of this place.'

Thorkill went forward and bowed to Gudmund, who invited him and his companions to follow him to his hall for dinner.

'But why do none of you speak but Thorkill?' asked Gudmund as they went on their way.

King Gorm merely shook his head, and Thorkill made haste to explain:

'Noble Gudmund,' he said, 'it is for very shame that my friends speak never a word. They know little of your language, with which I am so familiar, and are ashamed to struggle with a speech that they do not know – or to speak in a tongue which is foreign to you.'

So they came into the hall, and took their places at the tables with Gudmund's twelve handsome sons and many lovely daughters.

'Why do none of your companions either eat or drink what is set before them?' asked Gudmund suspiciously.

'Ah!' said Thorkill readily. 'That is wisdom on our part. We have been long at sea, feeding on the simple food of sailors. If we touched the rich and wondrous meats of your land I fear that we should suffer in our health. For this reason only do we eat our own food – and not out of discourtesy, or thinking any scorn of the truly wonderful things which you have set before us.'

This baffled Gudmund; but presently he made another attempt to entrap his guests. He instructed his lovely daughters that they were to offer themselves in love to their noble visitors.

Remembering Thorkill's words, King Gorm frowned warningly at his followers, and Thorkill made haste to explain to Gudmund that the King and all his followers were married men, and it would be disloyal to their wives, according to the custom in Denmark, even so much as to kiss any other woman.

Nevertheless three of the Danes found the daughters of Gudmund so beautiful that they could not refrain from kissing them – and immediately madness seized them, and they were never in their right wits again.

Seeing how successful this lure had been, Gudmund then invited his guests to visit his beautiful garden and gather any fruit they might wish.

But Thorkill excused himself and the king and his followers, saying that they must hasten on their journey and could not stay even to see the gardens which he was sure were even more beautiful than he had heard they were.

Gudmund then realized that Thorkill understood the dangers of the place more fully than he had expected. So he tried no more treachery, but made haste to ferry his visitors across the river, directing them to Geirrodur's house.

In a little while they came to a strange, desolate city of Troll houses: stony mounds which could be raised up on red pillars when the Trolls wished to let light into their dark dwellings. Over the city hung a cloud of dirty smoke, and here and there heads stuck on poles grinned horribly at the visitors.

As they passed through the city, the Trolls slunk away from them like ghosts frightened by the light of day, and so they came to Geirrodur's castle.

As they approached fierce dogs came rushing out to attack them; but Thorkill flung horns smeared with fat for them to lick, and he and his companions reached the door of the hall in safety.

But there King Gorm's warriors paused and drew back in fear, for ghastly shrieks came floating out to them, together with a most terrible smell which almost stopped their breath.

Thorkill, however, encouraged them: 'You will be quite safe if you are careful and do exactly as I tell you,' he said. 'Above all, keep your hearts from covetousness: touch nothing you may see in the castle. Geirrodur will show you priceless jewels and wondrous armour, or it will be lying about ready for anyone to pick up. But let no one even touch anything, and then no harm can come to us.'

Then King Gorm marshalled his men in fours, and they marched boldly into the great hall where the fires glowed redly through the reeking smoke. It was a terrible place, the pillars grimed with soot, the walls plastered with filth, the floor covered with stinking dirt and crawling with snakes and loathsome worms. Seated on iron benches at either side huddled miserable-looking Trolls who seemed half dead.

On a stone chair sat Geirrodur himself, an old Giant with a great gash through his body, and behind him the rent pillar and the chasm in the rock. Beside him sat his daughters, all huddled up since their backbones had never mended again, and they were now hideous with sores and tumours.

Neither Geirrodur nor his daughters spoke, or even looked up; and King Gorm and his men were only too ready to turn and hurry out of that noisome place, while Thorkill reminded them how Thor had flung the white-hot iron through the Troll King and had broken the daughters' backs when they tried to crush him against the roof.

Suddenly, as they reached the hall door, they saw treasures laid out before them. There were barrels filled with jewels, belts of gold, the tusk of a strange beast tipped at both ends with gold, a huge stag's horn decked with flashing gems, and a large golden bracelet most beautifully decorated with jewels.

Then, forgetting all warnings, one man snatched up the bracelet and clasped it round his wrist; another stretched out quivering fingers and took up the horn; while a third could not resist raising the tusk and slinging it over his shoulder.

But no sooner was the bracelet clasped in place than it turned into a snake and bit the man who had taken it with its poisoned fang; the horn lengthened out into a serpent, twined round the thief, and laid him dead on the floor; while the tusk turned suddenly into a sword and plunged through the body of the man who held it.

In terror the rest of the warriors turned to rush out of the castle; but before they had passed the gate they came to an open door, and looking in they saw that it was Geirrodur's treasure chamber. There lay rich cloaks and belts, golden helmets and wondrous weapons, many of them too large for ordinary men to wield.

At the sight even Thorkill forgot his wisdom, and he reached forth his hand and picked up a rich, warm cloak. King Gorm and his men also began to take things, and would have loaded themselves with plunder. Then on a sudden the room seemed to shake, and there was a scream of 'Thieves! Thieves!'

The Trolls, who had seemed more dead than alive before and certainly as harmless as if they had been turned into stone, suddenly attacked from all sides. A furious battle raged, and King Gorm and all his men would have been killed if the brave warrior Buchi had not shot fast and well with his bow and kept back the Trolls until the King was out of the city. Even so only twenty men escaped, and with King Gorm and Thorkill, Buchi and his brother, hastened down to the riverside where they found Gudmund waiting for them with his boat.

He ferried them across the river in safety, and took them back to his house.

In the morning they made ready to set out overland towards where their ships were waiting for them. But then they found that brave Buchi the archer was lost to them. For he had fallen in love with one of Gudmund's daughters who had tended him after the battle, and asked her to be his wife. She had accepted: but no sooner did they seal their betrothal with a kiss than Buchi's brain began to whirl, and by the morning he had lost his memory and was raving mad.

Sadly King Gorm and Thorkill set out from Gudmund's hall, reached their ships in safety, and sailed away. But even then they had storms to endure on their way down the Vimur river and across the seas, so that few indeed of them came back to Denmark.

And after that not even Thorkill the great traveller dared ever again to visit that fearsome land where Geirrodur the Troll King sat in his loathsome castle, maimed and silent from the terrible blow which Thor had dealt him.

10

THE CURSE OF ANDVARI'S RING

While it was still the custom of Odin to wander through Midgard in disguise, he came one day in company with Honir and Loki to a beautiful river which ran swiftly through a deep valley.

As they followed it up towards its source they found a big waterfall in a deep and solitary glen; and on a rock beside the fall they saw an otter blinking its eyes happily as it prepared to eat a salmon which it had caught.

Loki at once picked up a stone and flung it at the otter with such good aim that a moment later it lay dead upon the dead salmon.

'Ah-ha!' cried Loki. 'Two at a blow! Trust me to get both an otter and a salmon with one stone!'

He picked up his double catch, and the three Æsir went on again until they came to a house set in the midst of rich farm-lands and walled about strongly as if it were the home of some great lord.

The three travellers came up to the gateway, and finding it open, went in to the great hall where sat a dark man with flashing eyes alone on a seat beside the fire.

'Greetings, strangers!' he cried. 'Tell me who you are and why you come hither to the hall of Hreidmarr the master of magic?'

'We are poor pilgrims journeying through the world,' answered Odin, doffing his broad-brimmed hat politely as he leant on his staff and surveyed Hreidmarr with his one eye, 'and seeing your strong house set amidst such fruitful fields of corn, we turned aside to visit you.'

'Poor though we may be,' added Loki quickly, 'we are strong and clever in our own ways. Look here at this otter and salmon which I laid low with the cast of a single stone!'

When he saw what Loki carried in his hands Hreidmarr rose to his feet and shouted:

'Come hither, my sons Fafnir and Reginn! Come and bind these evil men who have slain your brother Otter!'

Then, while he held them powerless by his magic, two strong youths came into the hall and bound them securely with iron chains.

'And now,' said Hreidmarr grimly as he sat gloating over his three captives, 'it remains only to decide how you shall die.'

'For what reason would you kill us?' asked slow Honir, hoping to win out of danger by the smooth power of argument.

'You must know,' answered Hreidmarr, 'that I am a master of black magic such as is known among the Trolls and Swart Elves. And my three sons share my art, but in addition have the power of changing their shapes at will. My eldest son Otter chose to pass his time in the shape of an otter so that he might catch the fish in which he delighted as they sprang down the waterfall not far from here which is called Andvari's Force. The otter which you slew is this very son of mine, and justice demands a life for a life.'

'But justice allows also of wergild,' Honir replied stolidly, 'that is a payment for a slaying if it be done by chance. My companion here flung a stone at what seemed but a common beast of the riverside. Come now, decide on the wergild that shall pay for the death of your son.'

Then Hreidmarr consulted with Fafnir and Reginn, and at last he said:

'Strangers, we will take wergild, and it shall be this: enough good red gold to fill the skin of the otter which was my son, and to cover it so that not a hair may remain showing. Two of you shall stay here in chains, while the third goes forth to fetch the golden payment.'

The three Æsir consulted apart, and the end of it was that cunning Loki was sent out to find the golden ransom. 'Go to the Black Elves and to the Dwarfs,' Odin instructed him. 'Use all your arts, for we are in the hands of wizards who must not know who we are. Therefore I cannot send to Asgard for help.'

'Depend upon me,' answered Loki with a cunning smile. 'I know where the gold is to be got – though it will indeed require all my arts to win it for our use.'

So, while Odin and Honir remained in chains, and Fafnir and Reginn skinned the dead otter to measure out the wergild, Loki set forth in search of treasure.

He went straight back to Andvari's Force, from which the otter had taken the shining salmon, and sat himself down beside the rushing waters.

Loki could see through the roaring arch of green and silver, and presently he perceived Andvari the Dwarf in the likeness of a pike hiding in the mouth of his cave which was behind the waterfall; and there was a glimmer of gold in the darkness of the cave behind him.

'How can I catch him?' thought Loki. 'I could never take him with my hands, and he is far too wise to be caught by any hook however cunningly I might bait it . . .'

Then Loki thought of Ran, the cruel wife of Ægir, the Giant who ruled the Sea, who caught shipwrecked sailors in her net and drew them down to the bottom of the ocean. Ran was not friendly to the Æsir, but she recognized the evil Giant blood in Loki, and willingly lent him her net.

'But do not let the Æsir see it,' she warned him, 'nor yet the men who dwell in Midgard. For a day may come when you will wish to escape, and only a net such as mine could snare you.'

Loki took Ran's net and returned to Andvari's Force. There he cast it into the water and drew it up so smartly that the great pike was entangled in its meshes and lay gasping on the bank.

Loki grasped him in his hands and held him until Andvari returned to his own Dwarfish shape and asked sulkily what he wanted.

When Loki told him, Andvari to save his life was forced to give up all his treasure. He carried it up out of the cave behind the arch of falling waters and stacked it on the bank – and it was a very great pile indeed, such a treasure of rich gold as had never before been seen in Midgard.

When at last it was all there, Andvari the Dwarf turned sulkily away. But as he did so he put out his hand and swept quickly under it one little golden ring.

Watchful Loki saw this, however, and sternly bade him fling it back on to the pile.

'Let me keep just this ring,' begged Andvari. 'If I have it, I can make more gold: but the charm will not work for any who is not of the Dwarf race.'

'Not one scrap shall you keep,' said Loki viciously, and he snatched back the ring and held it firmly in his own hand.

'Then,' answered the Dwarf, 'take with it my curse. And know that the curse goes with the ring and brings ruin and sorrow upon all who wear it until both ring and gold come back into the deep waters.'

So saying Andvari turned himself into a pike once more and dived to the bottom of the river.

But Loki collected the gold and carried it back to Hreidmarr's dwelling where Odin and Honir were waiting anxiously for him.

When they saw the gold, Hreidmarr filled the otter skin full of it and set it up on end. Then they piled gold round it until the skin was completely hidden – and the gold was all used up.

As the gold was being stacked, Odin noticed Andvari's Ring and it seemed so fair to him that he took it out of the pile and slipped it on to his own finger. When the gold was all heaped up, he exclaimed:

'Now, Hreidmarr, our wergild is paid. See, the skin of the otter is altogether hidden under the gold.'

Hreidmarr examined the heap carefully.

'Not so!' he exclaimed. 'One hair on the snout is still showing. Cover that also, or the wergild is not paid and your lives are forfeit.'

With a sigh Odin took the ring from his finger and covered the last hair with it; and so the wergild was paid and they were set at liberty.

When they were free, and Odin held his spear once more and there was no longer any danger, Loki turned to Hreidmarr and said:

'With the ring of Andvari goes Andvari's Curse: evil and sorrow upon all who wear it!'

Then the three Æsir returned to Asgard. But they left behind them the curse of Andvari's Ring which had already begun to work on Hreidmarr and his two sons.

'You must give us some part of the wergild,' Fafnir and Reginn told their father. 'Otter was our brother as well as your son.'

'Not one gold ring shall either of you have,' answered Hreidmarr, and he locked up the treasure in his strongest room.

Then Fafnir and Reginn made a plot together, and the end of it was that Reginn murdered their father Hreidmarr for the sake of Andvari's gold.

'And now,' said Reginn when the evil deed was done, 'let us share the treasure between us in equal portions.'

'Not one gold ring shall you have,' answered Fafnir. 'Little do you deserve it indeed, seeing that you slew our father for its sake. Now go hence speedily, or I will slay you also! A life for a life is the law: and your life is forfeit for the murder of Hreidmarr.'

So Fafnir drove Reginn away, and he himself set Hreidmarr's Helmet of Terror on his head and carried all the treasure which had been Andvari's hoard to Gnita Heath far from the haunts of men

and hid it in a cave. Then he took upon himself
the form of a terrible dragon and lay down upon
the gold and gloated over it after the custom of
dragons.

But Reginn, vowing vengeance in his heart,
went to the court of Hialprek, King of the Danes,
and became his smith. There he received into his
charge the young hero Sigurd the Volsung, the
son of Sigmund to whom once on a time Odin
had given a magic sword.

For once in the hall of King Volsung, as all the
warriors sat over their mead, a stranger came out
of the darkness, a one-eyed man wearing a long
cloak and a broad-brimmed hat. Up the hall he
went until he came to the trunk of the great oak
tree round which the hall was built.

When he reached it the stranger drew a great,
shining sword and plunged it into the hard wood
so that it sank to the very hilt.

'Who so draweth this sword from this stock,
shall have it as a gift from me, and shall find that
never a better sword was borne in hand by mortal
man in Midgard!' he cried.

Then he went out from the hall and vanished
into the night: and King Volsung and his warriors
knew that their visitor had been Odin.

When he grew up Sigmund, Volsung's son, was
alone able to draw the sword out of the tree; and
many mighty deeds he did with it, for none could
stand against him.

At last, however, the day came when Sigmund

was fated to die. As he fought his last battle he found none who could withstand him, till Odin came suddenly against him in his blue cloak and broad-brimmed hat and caught the swinging sword against the staff which he carried in his hand. At once the sword blade broke into pieces, and very soon afterwards Sigmund fell mortally wounded.

All the race of the Volsungs were killed in that battle except King Sigmund's wife Hiordis. When the battle was over she went amongst the slain and found her husband yet living. With his last breath he bade her take the pieces of the sword and keep them carefully.

'For when our son is born,' he gasped, 'he will become the noblest and most famous of all the Heroes of Midgard. From the pieces of this sword shall be made another weapon called Gram, and greater deeds shall Sigurd do with it than ever I performed.'

Then Sigmund died, and presently Hiordis became the wife of King Hialprek, who proved a kind and generous stepfather to young Sigurd.

Reginn was made his guardian and tutor, and he taught him well and honestly all those things which a warrior should know. He did, however, try to make him discontented with his lot, for he did not wish Sigurd to remain quietly in Denmark: but he did not succeed in turning him against his stepfather or his adopted home.

'Surely you know how much wealth your father

had?' said Reginn. 'Why, he was a king, and yet you are content to be without importance in your stepfather's house.'

'I am not without importance,' answered Sigurd. 'I have but to ask and I shall receive.'

'You must prove that,' replied Reginn. 'Ask the King for a horse, the best that he has – and see what happens!'

'He will grant it!' cried Sigurd hotly. 'Willingly! And anything else for which I ask!'

Nevertheless he went to the King and asked for the gift of a horse.

'Take whichever you like,' answered the King, 'and anything else of mine no matter what it be.'

Next day Sigurd went to the wood where the royal horses grazed to choose one for himself. As he went he met an old man with a white beard and only one eye, who wore a long blue cloak and a broad-brimmed hat.

'Whither away, young sir?' asked the old man.

'I come to the wood to choose a horse for myself,' answered Sigurd. 'But you, honoured sir, seem old and full of wisdom: advise me, I beg, how to choose my steed.'

'Come with me,' answered the old man, 'and we will drive them into the swift waters of the Busil Tarn.'

They did so, driving the horses down a steep bank into the swift river. Then all of them were afraid and turned back to the land except one horse, a great grey stallion young and fair to see, on which no man had yet ridden. And this horse Sigurd chose.

Then the old man said: 'From Sleipnir's kin is this horse come: you must tend him well, for he will be the best of all horses,' and having said this he vanished, and Sigurd knew that it was Odin.

Sigurd led home the horse, which was called Grani, and soon became a good and fearless rider.

Seeing that he was now full grown, and a man of great strength and courage, Reginn told him about the dragon Fafnir who lay upon the great hoard of gold in the cave on Gnita Heath.

'So large and fierce is that dragon,' ended Reginn, 'and so deadly is the poison which pours from his mouth, that no man has dared to go up against him to slay him and take the treasure.'

'If I had but a good enough sword,' cried Sigurd, 'I myself would venture against the dragon Fafnir and seek to be his bane!'

'I will make you a sword,' answered Reginn the master smith, and he went to his forge and fashioned a shining blade which he gave to Sigurd.

'Behold your smithying, Reginn!' cried Sigurd, and he smote the anvil with the sword so that the blade was shivered into fragments. 'Go, forge me a better!' he said, and flung down the handle.

Then Reginn put all his knowledge and cunning into the forging of a fresh blade, and he brought the new sword to Sigurd who gazed on it with admiration.

'Maybe this will satisfy you,' Reginn said,

'though you are indeed a hard task master for any smith.'

Sigurd smote the anvil with the new sword, and once again the blade broke into pieces and he flung down the hilt, crying:

'It seems that you are but a liar and an evil smith. Or maybe you would betray me to this dragon Fafnir who, as I have heard tell, is your own brother!'

Then Sigurd went to his mother Queen Hiordis and said: 'Have I heard aright that my father King Sigmund gave you the good sword Gram, the gift of Odin, in pieces?'

'That is true enough,' she answered.

'Then give me the pieces, I pray,' said Sigurd, 'for I would fain have a sword that is worthy of my father's son.'

So she gave him the pieces of the sword Gram, saying that he would win great fame with it, and he carried them to Reginn and bade him make a sword.

Reginn took the pieces into the smithy, cursing Sigurd under his breath. But he put all his skill into the re-making of Gram: and as he carried out the finished work it seemed to him that fire burned along the edges of the blade.

Sigurd took the sword, and it seemed good to him. But nevertheless he whirled it up and struck the anvil with all his strength; and the keen blade cut through the iron anvil and down into wooden stock beneath without so much as blunting the edge.

'This is indeed a fine sword,' said Sigurd. But as a last test he went to the river and flung a lock of wool upstream. Then he held the sword in the water so that the lock was borne down against the sharp blade, and it was cut in half when it touched the sword.

'And now,' said Sigurd as he girded the sword Gram to his side, 'I am ready to go forth against the dragon. But first I must avenge my father's death, for such is my sacred duty.'

Sigurd was so well loved by man, woman, and child among the Danes that a band of warriors immediately gathered to follow him. So he sailed over the sea to attack the folk who had slain his people the Volsungs; he defeated them in a battle, and killed King Lyngi, who had brought about Sigmund's death, with a single blow of the sword Gram.

After he had been at home for a little while, and had been feasted as a hero by the great ones among the Danes, Sigurd remembered the dragon Fafnir.

So he went to Reginn the master smith and said:

'Fafnir the dragon has been in my memory all this while. Lead me to Gnita Heath and show me how I may come to him.'

Sigurd and Reginn rode away into the wilderness and came at last to the river at which Fafnir was wont to drink. And there was a long track down over the heath from the cave where the dragon dwelt.

'You told me that this dragon was no bigger than others of his kind,' said Sigurd. 'But now that I see his tracks, I can guess that he is by far the greatest of all dragons.'

'Yet you may kill him,' answered Reginn, 'if you will but dig yourself a hole in the path and stab him to the heart as he passes above you on his way down to drink at the river.'

'But what will happen if the blood of the dragon falls upon me?' asked Sigurd.

'It is no use for me to offer you advice,' exclaimed Reginn, 'if you are afraid of every danger. Truly you are not worthy to be called the son of Sigmund.'

Then Sigurd rode forward towards the cave, but Reginn went and hid in the rocks by the river, for he was very much afraid.

Sigurd began to dig the pit in the dragon's pathway; but while he worked there came to him an old man with a long white beard who had but one eye under his broad-brimmed hat, and asked him what he was doing.

When Sigurd told him, he said: 'You are following the advice of one who wishes you evil. Rather you should dig many pits and trenches, and hide in one where the blood cannot come to you after you have thrust your sword into the dragon's heart.'

Then the old man vanished, and Sigurd did as he was told, and afterwards lay hidden in one of the pits.

At last the time came for the dragon to take his morning drink, and the earth shook under his tread while he snorted forth venom as he went.

Sigurd neither trembled nor was afraid of the dreadful roaring of the monster nor of the steaming venom. But as the beast passed over the pits Sigurd thrust the sword Gram under its left shoulder and up to the very hilt. Then he leapt back, withdrawing the sword as he went, and slipped out by the trench at the side.

When Fafnir realized that he had his death-wound, he lashed out with head and tail so that all things within reach of him were broken to pieces. Then, knowing that his death was upon him, he lay still and asked:

'What mighty hero is it that has smitten me? What son of what famous father is so bold as to come against me sword in hand?'

Sigurd, knowing how dangerous the curse of a dying man could be, made answer:

'Unknown to men is my kin: I am called but a noble beast!'

Then Fafnir said: 'Reginn my brother has brought this about, and it gladdens my heart to know that he is at your side; for I know well how he is minded. And now I know you for Sigurd the Volsung that shall be called Fafnir's Bane for my slaying. Take my gold, but remember that it will itself be the bane of everyone so ever who owns it, even as it has been mine. For the curse of Andvari is upon it.'

After this Fafnir the dragon rolled upon the ground and died, nor even in death did he regain his human shape.

Then came Reginn to Sigurd and said: 'Hail, lord and master! A noble victory have you won in slaying Fafnir against whom none else dared stand. Yet he was my brother, and I too am guilty of his death, so I beg of you do this for me, that the blood-guilt may pass from us: cut out the heart of the dragon and roast it with fire, and let me eat it. Then all the guilt shall be mine, and no blame rest upon you, who have but slain a dragon and no more.'

Sigurd did as he was asked, and while Reginn went apart and rested in the deep heather, he set the dragon's heart on a rod and roasted it before a fire.

After a while Sigurd touched the dragon's heart with his finger to see if it were yet roasted, and the hot gravy burnt his finger so that he put it quickly to his mouth. The moment the heart's blood of the dragon touched his tongue, he straightway understood the speech of all the birds. And he heard how the woodpeckers chatted together in the trees nearby:

'There sits Sigurd,' said one of them, 'roasting the dragon's heart for another. But if he ate it himself he would become the wisest of all men.'

'There lies Reginn,' said another, 'planning to murder Sigurd and steal all the gold of Andvari's hoard for himself.'

And a third said: 'Why does not Sigurd strike off that traitor's head and win the gold for himself?'

'Why not indeed?' exclaimed Sigurd springing to his feet. 'Let Reginn go by the same road as Fafnir his brother!'

Then he drew the sword Gram and smote off Reginn's head. After which he made his supper of dragon's heart, and lay down to sleep upon the gold of Andvari's hoard in Fafnir's cave. But first of all he placed Andvari's ring upon his finger.

In the morning as he was loading the treasure upon Grani's back he heard the birds singing a new song:

'High upon Hindfell   the shield-hall rises;
Without, all around it,   sweeps red flame aloft.
Therein bideth Brynhild   bound by the sleep-
   thorn,
The loveliest lady,   this land ever knew.
If Sigurd should seek her   sleep shall be ended –
By Odin ordained –   shall be ended for him.'

At that Sigurd leapt upon Grani's back and rode forth towards Hindfell; and after a while he saw a great light burning upon the mountain top. On and on he rode until, on the heights of Hindfell, he came to a wall of fire surrounding a hall made of shields with a banner floating above it.

Sigurd set spurs to Grani and leapt through the flames without taking any harm. Then he dismounted and strode into the shield-hall.

There he found a figure in golden armour lying as if dead. He plucked at the helmet, but the armour seemed to be growing to the figure, so that he was forced to cut it away. The tough rings parted before the keen blade of Gram as if the armour were made only of cloth.

Then Sigurd saw that the warrior who lay inside it was a lovely maiden with golden hair who slept peacefully, growing no older nor needing either food or drink.

He bent down to kiss her, and as he did so he saw a thorn sticking into her flesh. He drew it out, and she awoke slowly from her magic sleep and looked up at him.

'Ah!' she murmured. 'You must be Sigurd the dragonslayer, for you wear Fafnir's Helmet of Terror upon your head even as it was foretold. Indeed I can see that you are the bravest and most goodly of men, with hair of golden-red, broad-shouldered and keen-eyed, and fair of speech.'

'Lady,' said Sigurd, 'you have named me aright. Sigmund was my father, the son of Volsung, and I am Sigurd, also called Fafnir's Bane, since I have slain that dragon and bear away Andvari's hoard which he guarded. But who are you? And why do you rest here in this charmed sleep, with a wall of fire burning ever about you?'

Then she answered: 'I am Brynhild, a mighty king's daughter. I was a Maiden of Odin, one of the Valkyries who follow his wild hunt and go out in the day of battle to summon to the Hall of

Valhalla those whom he has chosen to die. It chanced that on a day two kings fought, an old man and a young. Odin had promised the victory to the ancient one, and sent me to bring death to the other. But I broke the command of Odin and slew the ancient king in his place. For that deed Odin decreed that I should be a Valkyrie no longer, but must marry and go my way to death as other women do. Yet he had pity on me and vowed that I should be won only by the bravest of all heroes, even Sigurd the Volsung. So he set this wall of fire about me, stuck the sleep-thorn into my flesh, and left me here until the day of your coming.'

Then Brynhild rose and brought Sigurd a cup of wine, in which they plighted their troth, and in token of his faith to her alone he set a ring on her finger. But the ring was Andvari's ring, and the curse fell upon Brynhild from that moment.

When the next morning was come, Brynhild awoke from sleep and she roused Sigurd, saying:

'Up, slayer of Fafnir! You must go forth into the world to win yet greater fame and wealth, and a kingdom over which I may be queen. And here I shall wait for you, knowing well that none but you can leap the wall of flame which is about my hall.'

Sigurd was sad at this, yet his spirit burned to do great deeds for Brynhild's sake. So he kissed her farewell, mounted upon Grani, and leapt once more through the flames and so went on his way down the slopes of Hindfell until he came to the land where Guiki was king.

'Who are you that come riding through my gates laden with treasure?' asked King Guiki. 'For none dare come here without the leave of my valiant sons Gunnar and Hogni.'

'I am Sigurd the Volsung,' was the answer, 'Sigurd the slayer of Fafnir.'

'Then be you welcome,' cried King Guiki, 'be even as one of my sons, and take from our hands whatsoever you will.'

So Sigurd remained for a while with King Guiki, and won great war-fame at the side of Gunnar and Hogni. But Guiki's daughter Gudrun loved him from the first moment she saw him, and began to pine with longing for him.

Sigurd had no mind for her, though she was a fair princess indeed: for his every thought was of Brynhild, and he would often speak of her beauty and of the love that was between them.

Then Gudrun's mother, the Witch Queen Grimhild, made a magic drink and carried it to Sigurd as he sat in the hall one night. And he drank it, thinking it was but the cup of mead which it was the custom of the ladies of the house to bear into the hall after dinner. But as soon as it had passed his lips, its evil magic clouded his wits so that he forgot Brynhild and the love that was vowed between them; and it was to him as if they had never met.

Time passed, and soon he came to love Gudrun,

and presently they were married, and lived together happily. And Sigurd made a compact of
sworn brotherhood with Gunnar and Hogni.

So several years passed, and then Grimhild
decided that her eldest son Gunnar must win to
wife the lovely Brynhild who still dwelt in her
shield-hall ringed by flame on Hindfell, and whose
fame was growing among men throughout all the
lands thereabouts.

So Gunnar set out for Hindfell, and Sigurd and
Hogni went with him. When they came to the
wall of fire, Gunnar set his horse against it and
lashed him hard; but the horse drew back in
terror.

Then said Sigurd: 'Why do you give back,
Gunnar?'

And Gunnar answered: 'My horse fears the
fire. But lend me Grani, your great steed, and I
will leap it.'

'Yes, with my goodwill,' answered Sigurd, remembering nothing of his own visit to Brynhild.
Gunnar mounted Grani and urged him against
the wall of fire. But Grani snorted and drew back,
feeling an uncertain hand upon his bridle.

'Now we must bring magic to our aid,' said
Gunnar, who had been well taught by his mother.
And forthwith he practised shape-shifting so that
he wore the likeness of Sigurd, and Sigurd his.

Then Sigurd, seeming to all who saw him none
other than Gunnar, leapt upon Grani and sprang
easily over and through the flames, and came to

the shield-hall where Brynhild had sat for five long years waiting for her love.

'What man are you?' she asked, her eyes wide with dread.

'I am Gunnar, the son of Guiki,' was the answer. 'And I have come through the flame-ring which surrounds you, and so according to your oath you must be my wife.'

Then, since there was no help for it, Brynhild consented to this, and vowed herself to be Gunnar's wife. But that night as they slept in the shield-hall the sharp sword Gram lay between them as a token that the wedding was not yet. For in the morning the false Gunnar arose, drew a ring from his finger and set it upon Brynhild's: but in exchange he took from her finger Andvari's ring, and placed it upon his own.

Then he mounted Grani and leapt back through the fire. And when he was returned, he changed shapes once more with Gunnar, so that each had their right form.

Afterwards the flames died down and passed away, and Brynhild came out from her shield-hall on Hindfell, and when they came to Guiki's hall her wedding feast with Gunnar was held with much rejoicing.

But when Sigurd had Andvari's ring on his finger once more, the magic of Grimhild's brew began to pass from him, and in time he remembered all that had happened.

Then he was filled with sorrow and bitter

regret, for he knew that he still loved Brynhild above all women. But for honour's sake he made no sign and she was certain that he had forgotten what had passed between them, or that she had dreamed it, and that Gunnar was indeed the nobler and the braver of the two.

But one day when she and Gudrun were washing their hair in the river a dispute arose between them.

'As I have the braver husband of us two,' said Brynhild, 'it is my right to wash my hair further upstream than you.'

'But my husband is braver than yours,' answered Gudrun, 'so that it is I who can claim the right of the stream. For I am wedded to Sigurd who slew both Fafnir and Reginn, and won the rich treasure of Andvari's hoard.'

'It was a matter of far greater worth and valour,' exclaimed Brynhild, 'that Gunnar did when he rode through the flaming fire to win me, and Sigurd dared not.'

'And do you really believe that Gunnar rode through the flaming fire?' asked Gudrun scornfully. 'Now I think that he who won you, whatever form he wore, was he who gave me this ring, Andvari's ring, which I wear on my finger – and it was not Gunnar who won that ring by slaying the dragon Fafnir on Gnita's Heath.'

Then Brynhild was silent for she knew at last how she had been tricked and cheated, though she did not know why – and the curse of Andvari's ring was heavy upon her.

All that evening she was silent. But next day she told Gunnar that he was a coward and a liar, since he had never won her by riding through the flames, but had sent Sigurd to do it for him, and pretended that he had dared it himself.

'Never again,' she ended, 'shall you see me glad in your hall, never drinking, never playing at chess, never speaking words of kindness, never at my embroidery, nor giving you good counsel. No, rather shall I be plotting your death, for you have led me to break my vow – for well I knew that none but Sigurd could ride through the wall of flames that guarded my shield-hall. Oh, the sorrow of my heart that Sigurd might not be mine!'

Then she rent all her needlework and wept aloud so that all the house could hear her; for her heart was broken because she had lost Sigurd and married a man who was a coward and a liar.

At last Sigurd came to comfort her, begging her to love Gunnar her husband, and offering to give her all the treasure of Andvari's hoard if that would console her. But he would not desert Gudrun his wife, nor slay Gunnar his sworn brother – for to do either would be shame unspeakable.

'It is too late, too late to do anything: there is a curse upon us!' wailed Brynhild; and Sigurd grieved so at the loss of his one true love that his breast swelled mightily and burst asunder the iron rings of his shirt of mail.

But there was nothing he could do, and he went sorrowing back to his own dwelling. And Brynhild, mad with grief and shame and disappointment, urged Gunnar and Hogni with false tales to slay Sigurd.

They refused to do so, being mindful of their oath; but they commanded their young brother Gutthorn to slay Sigurd, and gave him a charmed drink so that he grew nearly mad with hate and cruelty.

But when he went into Sigurd's room, he shrank back and dared do nothing. A second time he went, and so bright and eager were Sigurd's eyes as they met his, that he dared not look at him. But he came a third time, and Sigurd was asleep. Then Gutthorn plunged his sword through his body and into the bed beneath, and turned and fled.

But Sigurd caught up his own sword Gram and flung it after Gutthorn so mightily that the keen blade cut him in half at the middle, and that was the end of him. But Sigurd the Volsung, the Slayer of Fafnir, fell back after his last great deed, and lay dead.

Then his body was placed on a heap of wood aboard his great ship of war, and it was set on fire and pushed out to sea. But before it left the shore Brynhild took the sword Gram and plunged it into her heart. Then she sank down beside Sigurd on the ship, with the sword lying between them, and the fire took both of them as the ship sailed into the distance.

Gunnar and Hogni, however took the treasure Andvari's hoard between them, and they gave their sister Gudrun as wife to a king called Atli. When Gudrun placed the ring of Andvari on Atli's finger the curse fell upon him too, so that he desired nothing more strongly than the gold, and cared not what evil he did to gain it.

So he invited Gunnar and Hogni to be his guests, and they came with a small train of followers. But before they set out, they hid the treasure Andvari's hoard deep beneath the waters of the river Rhine: and only they two knew the place.

When they reached Atli's hall, that evil king seized them, murdered their followers, and threatened them with torture if they did not tell him where Andvari's hoard was hidden.

Atli came first to Gunnar, who was set apart from his brother, and tried to make him tell where the treasure was hidden. But Gunnar said:

'Hogni and I have sworn never to reveal where the treasure lies, and I will not break my oath while Hogni lives. But bring me Hogni's severed head so that I may be sure that he lives no longer, and I will speak.'

Atli immediately caused this to be done, and when he saw the severed head of his brother, Gunnar laughed triumphantly.

'Now you shall never find Andvari's hoard!' he cried. 'Only we two knew its hiding-place, and my brother was weaker than I, and might have betrayed it. Now his lips are sealed for ever, and no torture will wring a word from me.'

Then in his rage and disappointment Atli had Gunnar thrown bound into a pit of serpents. But Gudrun sent her brother a harp, on which he played so wondrously well with his toes that no man had ever before heard the like. All the serpents fell into a doze, except one, which was not a true serpent but an evil witch in serpent's form: and she fastened her fangs in Gunnar's breast so that he died.

After this Gudrun, as was her duty, sought vengeance on Atli for the death of her brothers. In the end she destroyed him and his followers by setting fire to his hall and burning them all in it.

Then, wishing to live no longer, she flung herself into the sea. And so Andvari's ring, which was upon her finger, returned into the deep waters, and Andvari's curse was ended.

But Brynhild, who had once been a Valkyrie, rode in her chariot down the dark road to Nifelheim where Hela ruled the dead; and Sigurd was welcomed by Odin in Valhalla: for both of them were to play their part at Ragnarok, on the Day of the Last Great Battle.

11

Ægir's Brewing Kettle

While there was peace between Asgard and Jotun-heim, the Æsir held many glad feasts in their various halls. To them came even such Giants as had become their friends and acknowledged Odin as Allfather over the Nine Worlds.

Chief among these was Ægir, the Ocean Giant, who ruled over the sea and had the merciless Ran for his wife – Ran who had lent Loki the net with which she dragged sailors to their doom, so that he might catch with it Andvari the Dwarf to bring a curse upon the Volsung race whom Odin favoured.

Gaunt old Ægir with his white beard and green hair, and long, clutching claw-like fingers, seemed strange among the noble-looking Æsir and their beautiful wives. But his feasts in his own halls on an island in the Kattigat, where drowned sailors were welcomed as the dead warriors were in Valhalla, flowed with mead as plentiful as any in Asgard. And there his nine beautiful Wave-Daughters with their snow-white arms and breasts, their deep blue eyes and their flowing veils of green, followed their mother Ran with the golden cups even as Frigga's daughters did after the feasts in Asgard.

The Æsir had never visited Ægir's halls, however, until one day as a feast was ending in Asgard, loud-voiced Thor, his tongue loosened by much drinking, taunted their guest:

'Ægir!' he cried. 'You owe us Æsir many a feast in your halls: how soon will you begin to return all the hospitality which you have enjoyed in Asgard?'

The slow-witted old Giant took Thor's taunt as an insult. But he had both his excuse and his revenge ready.

'I have not presumed to invite the noble Æsir to my poor dwelling,' he said, 'for I fear that I could not feast them worthily. True, there is enough food and to spare for all of you: but alas, I lack a brewing kettle large enough to make sufficient ale or mead for all the Æsir at one time . . . For I know how much you, great Thor, are accustomed to drink. But if you can find me a kettle large enough, I here and now invite you all to feast with me at the end of harvest on my island of Hlesey ... But I fear that only among the Giants in Jotunheim is a big enough brewing kettle to be found.'

'I know of only one such,' said Tyr, the one-handed war-lord, slowly. 'My mother's father, the Giant Hymir, has a great host of kettles in his hall far to the eastward of the Elivagar river. One of them is a mile deep and so wide that you cannot see from one side of it to the other.'

'That brewing kettle I will get, if force or guile can do it!' cried Thor.

'And I will come with you,' said Tyr, 'for without me you will have but a sorry welcome from the Giant Hymir.'

So the two Æsir set out in Thor's goat-drawn chariot. The thunder roared and the lighting flashed from the wheels as they sped across the sky in a mighty storm-cloud, until they came beyond the Sleet Bays at the end of the heavens to the grim edge of Jotunheim nearest to Hymir's home.

At the last house in Midgard they left their chariot, and went foward on foot over the bare rocks and up the dark valleys, until they came to the huge stone hall where Hymir lived, not far from the edge of the ice-cold ocean.

At the door they were met by Hymir's wife, a terrible Giantess with nine hundred heads. She was about to seize the two Æsir, and Thor began to swing Miolnir ready to smite, when there came out another Giantess, fair and lovely to look upon, with hair shining like gold.

'Stay!' she cried. 'It is my son Tyr whom I bore to Odin the Allfather in the morning of time!'

At that the old Giantess went grumbling back into the darkness of Hymir's hall, while Tyr's mother welcomed the two Æsir beside the warm fire.

'I must hide you before Hymir comes,' she warned them. 'For he is sharp and savage to guests. You will be safe under a cauldron, until his anger cools; and when he knows that one of you is his grandson Tyr, I am certain that his rage will pass swiftly.'

Presently they heard slow, heavy footsteps in the distance, and quickly Thor and Tyr slipped under one of the cauldrons behind a stone pillar under the staircase.

Then Hymir came striding into the hall, the icicles on his beard tinkling and clattering together.

'Greetings, my father Hymir,' cried Tyr's mother. 'I beg you not to be angry, for we have guests who have come a long journey to visit us and borrow your great brewing kettle. One is my son Tyr, whom we have long hoped to see; and with him, in all peace and friendliness, has come his half-brother, the friend of man, who is named Thor.'

'Thor the Giant-killer!' roared Hymir, and he glared into the dark corner where the two Æsir were hiding. 'Where is Thor?'

The Giant's look was so piercing that the stone pillar split in two, and the great beam above it came crashing to the ground and broke in half. And down from the shelf over it came eight huge cauldrons, seven of which were smashed into pieces, leaving only the great brewing kettle unbroken.

Then the two Æsir came forward into the fire-light, and Hymir did not look kindly upon Thor when he saw him who had made widows of so many Giantesses standing in his own hall. But his first flash of rage had passed, and he thought it wise to welcome the Æsir as friends.

So he took three of his oxen, slew them, and set them to roast before the fire, while he gave his guests plenteous draughts of sweet mead and good home-brewed ale.

But he was rather surprised when Thor ate two of the oxen all to himself, leaving only one for the rest of the company.

'We must provide a larger feast than this for tomorrow,' he grumbled, 'or else we three shall go hungry, even if Thor is satisfied.'

So early next morning Hymir got up and went down to the sea-shore, dragging his boat after him, intending to catch a few whales for breakfast, in case his Æsir guests should eat up more of his oxen.

At the water's edge Thor joined him: 'Let me

row out to sea with you,' he said, 'for I should like to try my hand at fishing up monsters out of the deep.'

'You are not likely to be of much help in my fishing,' said Hymir scornfully. 'Your small size is against you: and certainly you will freeze if we stay out at sea for as long as my custom is.'

'Indeed!' cried Thor, angered by this insult. 'It seems to me that you are more likely than I to be the first who asks to row back.'

'Well, come if you must,' growled Hymir. 'But you'll have to find your own bait.'

'That will not be difficult,' exclaimed Thor, and springing over the wall into Hymir's meadow he seized his biggest and fiercest bull, a huge black beast called Heaven-bellower, and twisted off his head with a single flick of his wrist.

The Giant frowned, and muttered doubtfully to himself when he saw this, for he was frightened by Thor's strength, though he would not admit it even to himself.

So they got into the boat, and Hymir pushed off from the land while Thor sat down in the stern, seized a couple of oars, and rowed so lustily that Hymir felt more and more alarmed.

Very soon they reached the fishing-banks where Hymir was accustomed to anchor his boat and angle for flat-fish.

'We'll stop here,' he said, 'for the best fishing is always done at this distance from the shore.'

'Not so,' answered Thor, plying his oars until

they bent like withies. 'Here we would only catch miserable little fish. Only in the deep sea can we find monsters!'

Hymir became more and more uneasy, and at last he cried:

'Now we must indeed turn back, for here we are above the ocean depths where the Midgard Serpent rests.'

When Thor heard this he smiled grimly, and shipped his oars. Then he made ready a very stout line and a mighty hook, baited with the bull's head, which he lowered to the bottom of the sea.

Meanwhile Hymir was hauling up whales two at a time on his lines and flinging them into the boat in front of him.

'That's enough,' he exclaimed at last. 'Now let us row for the shore before any great danger befalls us.'

But even as he spoke, the Midgard Serpent snapped at the ox-head, and the hook caught in his jaws. When he realized that he was caught, he dashed away with such fury that Thor's fists holding the line crashed against the side of the boat.

With a roar of anger Thor braced himself against the pull and strained back so hard that his feet went through the bottom of the boat. But now, surely and steadily, he was drawing in his mighty catch; and the whole sea heaved and bubbled, and a great whirlpool opened round the line.

When the head of Jormungand came into sight above the water, Hymir cried aloud in terror: for nothing in the world could ever again seem fearful or hideous to those who had once seen the Midgard Serpent.

As Thor drew the monster to the side of the boat and made ready to strike it with his hammer, the whole earth shook; and the terrible cry of Jormungand echoed over the cold waters and away into the icy fastnesses of the north.

Hymir grew pale, his face turned yellow and his knees knocked together. At the very moment when Thor whirled up Miolnir to strike, Hymir lent forward and cut the line with his fish-knife; and the Migdard Serpent sank back to the bottom of the sea.

With a roar of rage Thor flung his hammer after Jormungand, and then smote Hymir on the side of the head with his fist so that the Giant plunged head first into the sea.

Miolnir returned to Thor's hand having done no more than bruise the Serpent's head; and Hymir clambered quickly back into the boat, where he sat sulkily, speaking never a word, while Thor rowed to land.

When they reached the shore, Hymir clambered out of the boat and said bitterly to Thor:

'I beg you at least to share the work with me. Either carry the whales to my house, or else pull the boat up on to dry land for me.'

'Right willingly,' answered Thor, whose gust of rage had already past. And he swung up the boat, complete with oars, bailer, bilge-water, and its cargo of whales and strode along the steep path to the Giant's house carrying it on his head.

They sat down to breakfast, and the whales very soon disappeared – mainly down Thor's ravenous throat.

Still, however, the stubborn Giant would not admit that Thor was stronger than he; and he decided to put him to one further test.

'Of course you can pull an oar strongly,' he remarked. 'And you fish well, besides carrying a boat fairly easily. But I can scarcely call you strong just for doing these things: for I do not suppose that you could break my beaker for all your strength. It takes a Giant to do even a little thing like that.'

Thor took up the Giant's beaker and looked at it. Then he flung it against a stone pillar so hard that it passed right through and crashed against the wall beyond.

But Hymir picked it up from the floor and returned it to him: and Thor perceived that it did not even show a dent in its surface.

Thor tried again and yet again, dashing it about with such force that it went through pillars and walls. But always when he picked it up it was quite whole and unmarked.

As he went to collect it for the last time, the beautiful Giantess, Tyr's mother, passed him and whispered swiftly:

'Dash it against Hymir's head! That is harder than any cup!'

Thor did as she suggested, and swinging round he hurled the beaker at Hymir's head with all his mighty strength.

The beaker fell to the floor shattered into fragments, while Hymir's forehead showed no mark. But the old Giant lamented bitterly the breaking of his favourite cup.

'Many good things are departing from me,' he sighed. 'Never again shall I quaff ale from this cup which now lies shattered at my feet . . . Well, Thor the Giants' Bane, and Tyr my grandson, you have prevailed. There stands my great brewing kettle: you have but to lift it and carry it away with you.'

Tyr at once stepped forward and seized the kettle: but strive though he might, he could not stir it.

Then Thor took it by the rim and swung it up so mightily that his feet sank though the floor of the hall. He clapped it on his head like a helmet and strode triumphantly away, the chains and pot-hooks rattling about his heels.

Along the road they went in the direction of the Elivagar river. But presently they heard a tumult behind them, and turning back saw a throng of many-headed Giants in pursuit, waving clubs and shouting that they would deal with all thieving Æsir who came into Jotunheim.

Thor set down the kettle, and swinging Miolnir round his head, hurled it at the nearest Giant who fell with his stone skull shattered in pieces. As soon as Miolnir returned to his hand, Thor threw it again: and so he continued until many of the Giants lay dead and the rest turned and fled back into the misty mountains of Jotunheim.

Then Thor clapped the kettle on his head once more and went forward full of pride and boasting of his feats among the Giants.

But when he came to the Elivagar river, the ferryboat was on the further side, and in it sat an old one-eyed ferryman with a hoary white beard and a broad-brimmed hat, wrapped in a dark blue cloak.

'How now, little old man across the river!' shouted Thor. 'Who are you, and why do you not bring the boat across for me?'

'Who is that churl of churls who shouts at me across the water?' answered the old man. 'Tell me your name, or never expect to be ferried across Elivagar. For Hildwolf the Giant, whose boat this is, has commanded me not to carry any poachers or thieves across the river, but only good men and worthy.'

'I am the Strong One of the Æsir,' answered Thor, 'and Odin is my father. Thor is my name – so you may well tremble.'

'As for me,' said the old man, 'my name is Hoarbeard. You must be an outlaw to pretend that you are Sif's husband! But even if you were really Thor himself you have a fiercer man to deal with now than you have ever met, since Rungnir's death!'

'I slew Rungnir the stone-headed Giant!' roared Thor. 'And what were you doing at the time of my great battle that makes you so boastful now?'

'Fighting five winters long in the All Green Island,' answered Hoarbeard, 'and gaining the love there of seven Giant sisters. Did Thor ever do the like?'

'I slew Thiassi,' was the answer, 'and tossed his eyes into the heavens where they now shine as stars. What say you to that?'

'Lebard was the sturdiest of Giants, yet I wiled him out of his wit and took his wand of magic. What were you doing then, Thor?'

'I was in the east of Jotunheim, smiting the ill-working Giant-brides on their way to the hills. Had I not slain them, the world would be teeming with Giants and no man could live in Midgard. What were you doing then, Hoarbeard?'

'I was in Valland, fighting for mankind, urging the heroes to stand against the evil ones. As for you, Thor, you were hiding in Skrymir's glove, shivering with fear lest the Giant should hear you.'

'Hoarbeard, you coward and dastard, I would smite you to your death if but my hammer would fly so far as to cross this river.'

'Why should you wish to kill me?' asked Hoarbeard. 'I speak only the truth. Have you done anything else to boast of?'

'I was in Jotunheim once, defending this river, when Svarang the Giant and his terrible sons set upon me. They pelted me with the tops of mountains, yet I defeated them, and they begged mercy of me in vain. What were you doing then, Hoarbeard?'

'I was in Jotunheim too, wooing a Giantess. Her son shall bring great help to the Æsir at the Day of Ragnarok.'

'I was slaying the wild women in the island of Hlesey —'

'Slaying women, a coward's game!' jeered Hoarbeard.

'These were witch-women; they went as werewolves!' shouted Thor. 'They shattered my ship with an iron club, and threatened to smite me, and kneaded my servant Thialfi as if he were dough. But come across the river, and I will soon show you with strokes of Miolnir if Thor is valiant.'

'I should never have believed,' answered Hoarbeard, 'that great Thor could be delayed on his homeward journey by a mere ferryman.'

'I will speak to you no more,' roared Thor. 'You utter nothing but evil, lying words. Be sure you will pay for them if ever we meet!'

'Take your boat then,' answered Hoarbeard, pushing it suddenly out into the stream, 'and go where the Trolls may get you!'

The boat sped across the wide river and came to where Thor and Tyr waited, though there was no one in it. And when they had entered and crossed to the further shore there was no sign of Hoarbeard the Ferryman.

So they went on their way to the place where the goat-drawn chariot was waiting for them, and drove swiftly back to Asgard. There Thor handed the brewing kettle to Ægir, who now had no excuse for not inviting the Æsir to feast with him.

And they all met in his halls at the Feast of Harvest Home, and agreed that even in Valhalla the mead and ale were not more plentiful, and that nowhere in Asgard was there more food served by such beautiful attendants as Ægir's lovely daughters the Wave Maidens.

But Thor was still sullen and moody since no one could tell him where he might find Hoarbeard the Ferryman.

'Were you not sitting on your Air Throne of Lidskialf when I strove to cross the river Elivagar?' he asked. 'Did you not see the ferryman, Odin my father? What were you doing at that time?'

'Bandying words with my boastful son Thor,' answered Odin, speaking suddenly in the voice of Hoarbeard the Ferryman. 'Now I am ready to pay for them, if Thor has learnt his lesson!'

Then Thor laughed until the thunder rolled round Midgard and the summer lightning flashed and flamed harmlessly over the broad Sound and the fair land of Denmark.

And none was merrier than he that night at the great feast in Ægir's halls.

12

THE DEATH OF BALDUR

During the happy days when the Giants made no open war against the Æsir, and the men of Midgard were mostly brave and noble warriors, Asgard was a place of kindliness and delight. And of all the palaces in that land of bliss none shone more brightly or sounded with more joyous laughter nor sweeter songs than Breidablik on the fair field of Ida where dwelt Baldur the beautiful, the fairest and the gentlest of all the Æsir, the best beloved son of Odin and Frigga.

Baldur's twin brother Hodur was as different as well could be, for he had been born blind, and was ever quiet and sad, sitting alone and brooding in his eternal darkness. Yet he was gentle and kind, and he and Baldur loved one another dearly. They would often walk together under the bright trees of Ida, the one golden-haired, with shining eyes and face alight with happiness; the other like a dark shadow lagging a little behind him, with black hair and pale, drawn face.

Baldur's palace had a roof of silver set upon pillars of rich gold, and was so pure and blessed that nothing common nor unclean could come within it. Here Baldur lived with his blossom-like wife, the sweet and delicate Nanna; and there was no more perfect love in all the Nine Worlds than the love of Nanna and Baldur.

Time passed even in happy Ida where Bragi would sing his sweetest songs and Iduna flit among the Æsir with her gleaming Apples, while Baldur went among them shedding light and happiness wherever he went.

In Midgard too men blessed bright Baldur: for he taught them the use of herbs and simples for healing wounds and other ills. The camomile flower was called Baldur's Brow because of its purity and its healing powers. Also Baldur understood the secret Runes which were engraved on the golden pillars of his house, and could foretell the future to men in Midgard.

But his own future he could not see, not could any of the Æsir; and the first shadow of coming sorrow came creeping over the golden fields of

Ida when Baldur ceased to smile and became grave and thoughtful as if his dark brother Hodur had come between him and the sun.

Then Odin and Frigga gathered the Æsir together in council, and they asked Baldur to tell them the cause of his silent grief, and why the light and joy had gone out of his radiant face.

Baldur replied: 'A strange trouble has come upon me. Hitherto I have always slept long and sweetly and all my dreams were of joy and happiness. But of late they have changed, have grown dark and terrible. Some danger draws near me, and death is at hand in a form unseen. I see the danger and the hand of the slayer, and I fly from it in vain down the long caverns of sleep; but when I awake I cannot remember the danger, and the face of my slayer is veiled from my sight. But the terror remains and the knowledge of doom which hangs over me – of the fate which draws nearer day by day, veiled and terrible, menacing in the darkness and hidden from my waking mind.'

The Æsir were sorely troubled at these words, and wise Odin who had drunk of Mimir's Well and spoken with the Norns themselves, grew sad. He knew that Baldur must die one day, and that his death would mean that Ragnarok was drawing near: but he did not believe that Baldur's day of doom would come for many a long age.

So, while the Æsir still debated in Gladsheim their high council hall in Asgard, Odin arose, saddled Sleipnir his eight-legged horse and rode away on the long path which led to Nifelheim.

Nine long nights and days he rode on fast Sleipnir down the dark ways and echoing caves; and he came at length to the River Gioll, the black stream which forms the edge of Hela's kingdom where the dead go who do not fall in battle.

Over the dark river stretched the Bridge of Gioll arched with crystal and paved with gleaming gold.

Seeing his eight-legged horse, the skeleton maiden Modgud who stood on guard there let him pass, though she asked him:

'Who of living men passes upon Odin's steed by the way of the dead?'

And Odin replied, speaking like an old man: 'My name is Vegtam the Wanderer, and I come by command of the Æsir who dwell in Asgard.'

'Pass, Vegtam the Wanderer,' answered Modgud, and Odin rode on through Iron Wood where the trees are black with leaves of sharp iron, until he came to the Gateway of Helheim where Garm of the bloody breast, Hela's great hell hound, bayed fiercely to keep in the ghosts of those who sought to escape back into the world of life.

But Odin did not try to enter Hela's halls. Instead he turned aside to the long grey barrow where the prophetess Volva the Wise lay buried. Standing beside her grave he began to chant the mighty spells which move the dead, until slowly

the earth gaped open and the form of the prophetess rose up above the barrow, wrapped in her
grave-clothes, her face green and ghastly.

Then the dead Volva spoke in cold measured
tones without moving her jaws or bending her
thin lips:

'What mortal, to me unknown, draws me back
by these weary ways?' she asked. 'I have been
buried under the snow, I have been washed by
the rain, the dew has drenched me. Long have I
been dead.'

Then Odin answered: 'My name is Vegtam the
Wise Wanderer: tell me now tidings of Helheim,
and I will tell you of Midgard if you wish to hear.
Tell me for whom Hela's benches are spread with
cloaks and her hall so fairly hung with painted
shields?'

'For Baldur the mead stands ready in Hela's
halls,' answered the dead Volva, 'and for him the
walls are decked with shields. Yet the Æsir still
make merry in Asgard and upon Ida's plain. All
unwillingly have I spoken: I will say no more.'

'Speak again, wise Volva,' commanded Odin,
'for I must learn all. Tell me, who shall cause the
death of Baldur? Who shall take the life of Odin's
best beloved son?'

'Hodur bears the branch of fate,' replied Volva.
'He shall cause the death of Baldur, and take the
life of Odin's best beloved son. All unwillingly
have I spoken: I will say no more.'

'Speak again, wise Volva,' insisted Odin, 'for I

must learn still more. Tell me who shall bring vengeance upon Hodur as the Norns command: who shall lift the slayer of Baldur on to the funeral pyre?'

'In the Halls of the West a son shall be born to Odin,' answered Volva. 'Vali shall be his name, and he shall slay the killer of Baldur. He shall neither wash his hands nor comb his hair until he has borne him to the funeral pyre. Before he is one night old he shall avenge Odin's best beloved son. All unwillingly have I spoken: now indeed I will say no more.'

'Speak once more, wise Volva', cried Odin desperately. 'When all weep for Baldur who is it that shall shed no tear?'

'Now I know that you are not Vegtam the Wise Wanderer,' answered Volva. 'You are Odin, for none other knows that question. Ride home now and seek to save Baldur from what fate decrees: for no other man shall behold me again until Loki breaks his chains and the Destroyers of the Æsir come at Ragnarok.'

Then Volva sank slowly back into the mound and the earth closed above her head.

Odin mounted Sleipnir and rode sadly back to Asgard, wondering how fate might be delayed or the web which the Norns had woven be changed to give Baldur longer life ... Wondering how Hodur could come to slay the brother whom he loved better than anyone in all the Nine Worlds ... Wondering how he might send Hodur away from Asgard or keep Baldur from his dangerous company.

But when he reached the heavenly mansions it was to find his wife the Queen Frigga sitting in Fensalir, her Hall of the Clouds, her eyes shining with happiness.

'Baldur is safe!' she cried. 'I have bound by an oath all things that grow out of the earth to do him no harm. And all things in the earth too – the rocks, the metals, and the soil itself; and all that dwells upon the earth, from the Æsir, the Giants, and the Trolls to the beasts and serpents; the birds of the air and all the creatures of the sea, besides the waves themselves. Yes, even the poisons and the sicknesses which can slay have sworn not to harm Baldur. So now our beloved son is safe.'

Then Odin was comforted. Although he knew that the doom must come, since the decree of the Fates could not be altered, he felt that now it must be a long time before the Norns could find a new means of death for Baldur.

Meanwhile the Æsir discovered that no weapon could hurt Baldur; and so a new game began in the sweet groves of Ida. First Tyr, it might be, would leap forward and swing his sword with his one strong hand as if to cleave Baldur in two: but the sharp blade would bend and whip back and Baldur was untouched. Or it might be Thor, fling-ing Miolnir with a shout; and the hammer which had slain so many Giants and shattered the stone head of Rungnir, returned to his hand without harming Baldur. Or again Uller the peerless Archer would loose arrow after arrow, and they would rebound as if Baldur wore invisible armour and drop to the ground without harming him.

Among the Æsir gathered round Baldur was Loki; and when he found that even in his hand no poisoned knife or wolf's tooth steeped in venom could harm him, the evil in his heart seemed almost to choke him. Suddenly he became all evil. He had always hated Baldur the beautiful, the good and stainless; now nothing mattered except to hurt him. All things in the world loved Baldur – all things but Loki; nor would even the vilest Troll nor the cruellest Giant hurt him; not even the stone by the roadside nor the snake in the grass.

Mad with jealousy and hate, Loki the unloved moved away from the happy crowd of Æsir in the shining fields of Ida, and began to plot and scheme as he had never plotted before.

Presently, as Queen Frigga sat spinning in Fensalir, her heart full of joy and thankfulness that Baldur was safe, there came an old woman hobbling with the aid of a stick, and greeted her.

'I hear sounds of joy and laughter coming from the glad fields of Ida,' said Frigga. 'Can you tell me what the Æsir do there which causes them such delight?'

'It is very strange,' mumbled the old woman. 'It is some sort of magic they practise. There stands Baldur laughing, and all the Æsir fling stones or shoot arrows at him, or smite him with their weapons. But nothing hurts him: the ground is littered with axes and swords, spears and arrows which have been used against him in vain.'

'Ah!' cried Frigga, her face lighting up with happiness. 'That is because no weapon can hurt Baldur! I have taken an oath from everything which lives or grows or moves upon the earth, everything that comes out of it or descends upon it or moves in the waters which touch it, that they will not harm Baldur.'

'And have all the trees and shrubs and plants and flowers and grasses really taken an oath not to hurt Baldur?' asked the old woman.

'Everything whatever it may be that grows out of the earth,' nodded Frigga.

'Westward of Valhalla,' said the old woman, 'there stands an oak tree, and from it grows a little plant called mistletoe. That does not grow out of the earth: has it also sworn not to hurt Baldur?'

'Indeed I did not think to take an oath from the mistletoe,' answered Frigga. 'It is so weak and soft and young, it surely cannot hurt anyone.'

'No indeed,' agreed the old woman. 'A foolish little plant that has no root of its own, but must lean on the oak for support, need not swear the oath, for it can hurt nobody.'

Then she bowed low to Frigga and hobbled slowly away, while the Queen of the Æsir bent forward to her cloud-wreathed loom once more. But now a vague shadow seemed to rest over her,

as if the Sun had passed behind one of the clouds
that she was spinning.

Outside Fensalir, Loki, in his own shape once
more, sped to the lonely oak westward of Valhalla,
and cut from it a sprig of mistletoe. Weak and soft
and harmless the pale green shoot appeared to be;
but Loki trimmed it and shaped it into a dart, and
then, muttering an evil Rune, he breathed upon it
and at once it was as hard and sharp as iron.

Carrying the mistletoe dart under his cloak Loki
stole back to Ida where the Æsir were still
gathered round Baldur flinging their useless
weapons at him. And there too a little band of
Trolls had come by special permission of the Æsir
and were hurling their stone hammers at Baldur,
screaming with laughter when they fell harmlessly
to the ground. There also might be seen a Dwarf
or a Black Elf carrying some cunningly fashioned
weapon made sharp and strong and unfailing by
some secret magic: yet even their magic could not
prevail against Baldur the world's darling.

Only blind Hodur took no part in the strange
sport. He leant against a tree nearby and listened
sadly to the joyous shouting and laughter.

'Why do you not shoot at Baldur?' asked Loki
the tempter stealing up beside him.

'I cannot see where Baldur is,' answered Hodur
with a sigh. 'And besides, being blind, I have no
weapon.'

'Ah, what a shame it is that you alone of all the
Æsir cannot do honour to your brother by casting

a harmless weapon at him,' said Loki. 'But if you wish it, I will place this little wand in your hand and guide you so that you may fling it at him.'

Then Hodur allowed Loki to place the mistletoe dart in his hand, directing his arm so that his aim might be true. And Hodur drew back and flung the dart with all his strength and it passed though Baldur's body, so that the Bright One fell dead to the earth. And that was the greatest mischance that has ever befallen among gods and men.

A deep silence fell upon the Æsir when they saw Baldur fall; and their hands dropped to their sides so that they could not even catch him as he fell. Each looked at the other, their eyes wide with horror, and when they tried to speak all burst out weeping so that no words came.

Only Hodur did not weep. He stood where Loki had left him, and his horror and his anguish were so great that no tears came.

The Æsir soon knew who had flung the fatal dart; and although Hodur had not meant to hurt Baldur, both they and he knew well that he must die – for such was the Law of the North which least of all might the Æsir break. Yet no one struck Hodur, for they were all sworn never to raise their hands against one another: moreover in the Plain of Ida and before the very palace of Breidablik no blood might ever be shed.

When the first numbing silence was over, and the first wild burst of weeping was stayed, Frigga spoke to the Æsir.

'Who among you all will win my favour and my love undying? Who will ride the road to Helheim and seek for Baldur, and learn if Hela will accept any ransom so that Baldur may come home to Asgard?'

There was silence for a little while, for the journey was difficult and the way very fearful.

Then Hermodur, the swiftest of the Æsir, who was their nimble messenger and Odin's chosen companion, sprang forward.

'I will journey through Nifelheim,' he cried, 'and come to the Halls of Hela, yes, and dare to enter her terrible gates, if thereby I can bring my brother Baldur back to the light.'

'Go then,' commanded Odin, 'and take Sleipnir my eight-legged steed to bear you swiftly on your way. For only I know quite how great a harm and loss the death of Baldur is to us in Asgard.'

So Hermodur drew on his shining armour, set his helmet upon his head, leapt upon Sleipnir, and was gone like a flash of lightning.

But the Æsir carried dead Baldur down to the sea-shore. There they drew out his longship Ringhorn, which was the greatest of all ships, and they launched it and moored it to the shore. Then they built a mighty funeral pyre upon it and laid precious jewels and rare embroideries upon the pyre.

Now, however, the ship was loaded so heavily that none could push it out into the sea. So they summoned the Giantess called Hyrrokin, who came riding upon a huge wolf with vipers for her bridle. She leapt from her steed, and Odin bade four of his most valiant Heroes from Valhalla to hold it: but they could not do so until they succeeded in flinging the wolf to the ground.

Then Hyrrokin went to the ship and thrust it out with one great heave, so mightily that the earth shook and the rollers on which it ran burst into flame.

Thinking she was insulting the dead, Thor grabbed Miolnir to crush her, but Odin made haste to calm his hasty-tempered son.

Then the body of Baldur was carried out and placed on the ship. And as sweet Nanna his wife bent weeping above him to kiss him for the last time, her heart broke, so that she died; and the Æsir placed her at his side, and the fire was kindled.

As Thor stepped back from kindling the fire, the tiny Dwarf called Lit dashed across in front of him, and Thor, still half-crazed with grief, kicked him aside, and he fell dead into the fire and was burned with the divine pair.

Now the burning ship was ready to sail out into the darkness, and the Æsir stood upon the shore watching it with tear-dimmed eyes. Nor did the Æsir mourn alone, for Frey drove his chariot along the shore from Vanaheim, and Freya too with the cats harnessed to her car. Odin and Frigga were followed by the Valkyries; and many of the Rime Giants came also, and other Giants out of Jotunheim; the Trolls came, and the Elves from Alfheim, and many a Dwarf from the caves under the earth.

As the ship left the shore Odin placed the ring Draupnir on Baldur's finger, and stooping he whispered the Word of Hope into his dead son's ear, the Word which all of the Nine Worlds longed to know.

Then as the ship moved away over the dark ocean, a low moaning cry rose and fell throughout the world. Far into the distance it went, and as it touched the horizon it seemed that sea and sky burned with it.

Suddenly it was gone, and darkness rushed in over the world like a black shroud of sorrow.

But Hermodur was riding on his way – nine nights and nine days through dark dales and deep – until he came to the burning river Gioll and on to the golden Gioll Bridge which crosses it.

'Who crosses this Bridge yet living, where none but the dead may cross?' cried Modgud the maiden of Death who guarded it. 'But yesterday five companies of dead men rode over, but the Bridge thunders no less under you alone, and, though living, you have the colour of a man already dead. Why ride you hither on Hela's road?'

'I am sent out of Asgard,' answered Hermodur, 'and I am appointed to ride to Helheim to seek out Baldur the beautiful. Have you perchance seen him passing this way into Hela's halls?'

'Over my bridge passed Baldur the beautiful with Nanna his wife,' answered Mogdud, 'and behind them ran a little Dwarf. They are in Hela's halls: downward and to the north lies Hel-way.'

Modgud stood aside for Hermodur to pass, and Sleipnir went wearily on the darksome road through Iron Wood until he came to Hel-gate where the great dog Garm of the Bloody Breast barred his way.

Hermodur dismounted from his steed and tightened his girths. Then he mounted again, set spurs to Sleipnir's sides, and the mighty horse leaped so hard and so high that he cleared the gate and landed far inside Helheim.

Onward to Hela's hall rode Hermodur, dismounted at the door, and strode inside. And there in the seat of honour sat Baldur his brother, while Nanna held the cup at his side and Lit the Dwarf waited upon them.

There Hermodur rested for the night, supping with Baldur in that chill abode of the dead; and in the morning he went onward to the great hall where Hela passed judgement on all who came to her realm.

Hermodur shuddered as he looked upon her ghastly face, half-living and half-dead; and he stood listening to the seething of the great cauldron Hvengelmir and the clashing of swords in the icy waters of the river Slid. He heard her judgements on the dead: he saw the wicked banished to Nastrond, the Strand of Corpses, where they waded in ice-cold streams of poison before they were cast into the cauldron Hvengelmir to serve as food for the terrible Nid Hog who would only pause from gnawing the roots of the Ash Yggdrasill to feed upon their bones.

He saw also the sadness and the gloom in the homes even of the virtuous who died 'a straw death' upon their beds; and he realized how much better it was to fall in battle and go to Valhalla where the dead heroes dwelt.

At last he himself knelt before Hela, and told her his errand – told her how great a sorrow there was among the Æsir, and among all living creatures, for Baldur's death, and begged that Baldur might be allowed to ride home to Asgard with him.

'Baldur may return to you,' said Hela in her cold even tones, 'if all things in the world, both quick and dead, weep for him. But if any fail to weep, then with Hela he remains.'

So Hermodur set out on his return journey most joyful at heart, and carrying back the Ring Draupnir as a gift from Baldur to Odin: for Hermodur was sure that nothing in all creation would fail to shed a tear so that Baldur might live again.

He came at last to Asgard and told all that he had seen and heard. Then the Æsir sent messengers over all the worlds praying that Baldur be wept out of Helheim, out of Nifelheim, and back into Asgard and the world of light. And besides the Æsir all mankind wept for Baldur and all living things as well. The earth itself wept too, and the stones, the trees and all metals – even as they still weep when they come out of frost into heat.

It seemed that everything created wept for Baldur: for even the Giants shed tears and forgot their age-old warfare with the Æsir.

Yet Baldur was still held in Helheim, and Hermodur rode near and far bidding all things weep, and weep again. Far and far into cold Jotunheim he went, and on a day he came to a cave where sat a solitary Giantess who did not weep.

'Who are you that do not weep for Baldur the beautiful?' asked Hermodur.

'I am Thokk,' answered the Giantess, 'and who is Baldur that I should weep for him?'

Then Hermodur told her about Baldur the beautiful, and of Hela's promise to release him if all things wept in sorrow at his loss.

But Thokk the Giantess laughed harshly: 'Thokk will weep waterless tears for Baldur!' she cried. 'Living or dead I care nothing for Baldur the son of Odin the churl. Let Hela keep what she already has!'

Over and over again Hermodur begged Thokk to weep, but all in vain. At last he turned sorrowfully away, leaving her still laughing, and rode back to Asgard.

When he had told his tale, Odin sat in silent sadness for a little while.

'Then Baldur must remain in Hela's halls,' he said at last, 'remain among the dead until the Day of Ragnarok – which I fear draws near us now . . .

As for Thokk the Giantess, it seems to me that she is none other than Loki, he who has wrought most ill among the Æsir – he who was our brother but is now our bitterest foe.'

13

VALI THE AVENGER

Baldur was dead, and the shadows were gathering
in Asgard. Care sat on the faces of the Æsir, and
Odin felt that Ragnarok had drawn suddenly
nearer. Yet even so the Day of the Last Great
Battle was still far in the future, while near at
hand lay the sacred duty of revenge.

Hodur, who had cast the fatal mistletoe must
die – for so the unchangeable law of gods and men
decreed, even though Hodur had cast his dart in
all innocence, meaning no harm to the brother he
loved so well.

None of the Æsir could slay him, however, on

account of their oaths; and moreover Hodur remained by day in Breidablik, mourning for
Baldur, and there least of all might a sword be
raised to kill. And at night when he wandered out
into the dark woods, none might see him to slay.

Odin, however, knew from the prophecy of
Volva that the Avenger was not yet born who
would slay Hodur. He knew also that it must be a
son of his whose mother was to be a mortal
woman, whom he must woo as a mortal, and that
the son was to be Vali, who would survive
Ragnarok.

But one thing which he did not know was who
his mortal wife was to be; and all his wisdom,
together with the wisdom of Mimir's Head, could
not tell him that.

At last he sent for his son Hermodur the swift
messenger of the Æsir:

'Put on your shining armour and your helmet,'
he commanded, 'saddle Sleipnir, and ride to the
uttermost north of Midgard. There you will come
to the Land of the Finns who, by their magic
powers, send down the cold storms over the world
of men. Among them dwells a wizard whose name
is Rossthiof, who, alone of all living men, can see
into the future. Go to him in haste and learn of
whom Vali the Avenger shall be born.'

Then the Valkyries buckled Hermodur's shining armour about him and handed him the tall
helmet, and he leapt upon eight-legged Sleipnir
and made ready to ride.

But Odin stopped him ere he set out. 'Remember,' he said, 'that Rossthiof is the most cunning and cruellest of wizards. It is his custom to draw innocent travellers to his ice-castle by magic arts, there to rob and slay them. Therefore take in your hand my runic staff: for without doubt when he learns that you come from me he will use all his evil art to overcome you or to drive you away.'

Hermodur took Odin's runic staff, and set out on his perilous mission. Over Bifrost Bridge he went where Heimdall sat on guard in his white armour holding the Giallar Horn in his hand to blow when the enemies of Asgard came in sight. Through Midgard went Hermodur, swift as the storm wind and the lashing rain: and here and there a man glimpsed him on his eight-legged steed, rubbed his eyes, and saw only the driving storm. Over the wild, mist-clad mountains he went, and the hail rattled round the hooves of Sleipnir, while avalanches thundered down into the deep valleys behind him.

At last he came to the dim land of eternal twilight near the northernmost point of the world where Rossthiof the Wizard had his castle of green ice. Then Hermodur knew that he was seen and that magic was at work: for Sleipnir seemed to be drawn forward across the ice as if by a magnet, and he could do nothing to stay him.

But Odin's wondrous steed was sure-footed as ever; again and again he paused suddenly and leapt cleanly over the hidden traps which

Rossthiof had laid for him – over crevasses in the ice covered thinly by crusts of snow; over drifts so deep that one false step would have buried horse and rider completely; and over loose masses of ice which, stepped upon, would have sent Hermodur and his steed rushing down the slippery mountain-sides to fall into chasms far below.

Presently there came grey and shadowy monsters, terrible in shape, threatening to crush them with many huge arms or bite them with gigantic teeth. But Hermodur rose in his stirrups and struck them with the runic staff which Odin had given him; and they shrank away and vanished moaning into the snow blizzards.

At last Rossthiof the Wizard came against him in the likeness of a Giant, swinging a great rope to bind both horse and rider. But as he drew near, Hermodur felled him with a blow of the staff and bound him with his own rope, drawing it so tightly round the wizard's throat that Rossthiof groaned in terror, and gasped:

'Messenger of Odin, I will speak and harm you no further, nor attempt to deceive you. What I show you now is true: I swear it by the black river of Helheim, the Leipter by which none in all the Nine Worlds dare swear falsely.'

Hermodur loosened the rope from about Rossthiof's throat and said:

'Speak then, Wizard of the North. Odin asks from whom shall be born Vali the Avenger who must slay Hodur.'

Rossthiof rose slowly to his feet and began to draw strange runes upon the frozen snow. After a while he held up his arms and began to chant terrible incantations. At their sound the sun was darkened, hiding her face behind black clouds; the earth shook and trembled, and the storm-winds shrieked and groaned with the voices of ravening wolves and of dying men.

'See!' cried Rossthiof suddenly, pointing with his long arm and thin blue fingers across the snow.

Hermodur looked and saw the mist roll back on a bare mountain top at a distance from him. Suddenly blood appeared upon the snow and seemed to flow down and redden all the ground. Then a beautiful woman rose out of the snow, holding a baby in her arms. Almost at once the child sprang to the ground and grew swiftly until he was a well-grown youth with a quiver on his back and a bow in his hands. He drew an arrow, fitted it to the bow and loosed it quickly: for a moment it flashed like fire, and then suddenly was buried in the darkness.

The mist came down again, and Hermodur saw nothing but the dim shapes of ice-bound hills, and frozen mountains rising grey and ghostly in the eternal Arctic twilight.

'What you have seen,' said Rossthiof, 'is the blood of Baldur staining the earth. Then Rinda came, the daughter of Billing, King of the Ruthenes. She is to be the mother of Vali who

shall shoot the arrow of vengeance and lay dark
Hodur low. Get you back to Asgard now, and tell
Odin that if he would be the father of Vali, he
must woo and win Rinda as a mortal man.'

Rossthiof turned and melted into the mist, growing large and terrible as any Giant as he strode
away into the darkness.

At once Hermodur sprang upon Sleipnir and
set out on his long journey back to Asgard; and at
last he knelt again before Odin and told his tale.

Then the Allfather of the Æsir rose from his
throne and laid aside his divine majesty. He went
down into Midgard with his broad-brimmed hat
drawn low over his brows to hide his missing eye.
His blue cloak was wrapped well about him, and
in his hand, instead of a staff, he held the spear
Gungnir.

In this guise he made his way to the West
where King Billing ruled, and offered his services
as a warrior well experienced in the arts of war.

King Billing was overjoyed, for at that time a
powerful enemy was about to invade his kingdom
with a large army.

'I have no general to command my forces,'
lamented King Billing, 'and I myself am too old
and infirm to march at the head of my men. If
only I had a son! But I have not even a son-in-
law, for my daughter Rinda refuses to marry. It is
not for want of suitors, for she is young and
beautiful: but she longs above all things to be one
of Odin's Maidens and ride with the Valkyries on

his wild hunt, so she despises and insults all men who come to ask her hand in marriage.'

'Old though I am,' said the disguised Odin, stroking his beard, 'I too may try my fortune with the beautiful Rinda. But first of all I must show my worth by leading your armies to victory.'

So Odin took command of King Billing's warriors and led them so well that the invaders were utterly defeated and never again dared to set foot in Ruthenia.

The mysterious commander inspired such courage in King Billing's men that no one seemed able to stand against them; and indeed he was said to have won the last battle quite alone by charging the foe single-handed, waving his spear – at which they broke and fled in terror.

King Billing had no suspicion of who his preserver was, and when the war was ended he called for him and said:

'Noble sir, to you I owe the victory, my crown – my very life. All that I have is yours: choose how I may reward you.'

'I ask but one thing,' answered the disguised Odin, 'and that is the hand of your daughter the Princess Rinda in marriage.'

'Though you seem old in years, I could ask for no better son-in-law,' answered the king. 'But alas, my daughter cannot be commanded. She is yours indeed – but only in you can win her.'

King Billing sent for Rinda, and she came to

the hall, as sweet and winsome a maiden as any in
the world.

'My daughter,' said the old king gently, 'this
noble lord who has defeated all our enemies and
saved us from conquest, death, and captivity, asks
only one reward – and that is your hand in marriage. It rests with you, for he has my full consent.
Surely you will reward the noble saviour of our
country?'

'Thus I answer him,' cried Rinda, 'and thus
only do I give him my hand!'

As she spoke she stepped forward and struck
Odin in the face.

Then, laughing disdainfully, she turned and
went back into her chamber and locked the door
behind her.

Odin, however, was not to be defeated in his
purpose. He said farewell to King Billing, who
was sad indeed to see him go, and set out once
more on his travels.

But very soon he was back again in Ruthenia,
disguised this time as Rosstheow the Goldsmith –
a broad, middle-aged man with a clever, distin-
guished face – but still only one eye.

He at once began to practise his craft, and was
soon famous throughout the land for the making
of beautiful shapes in bronze and gold, and for the
wondrous ornaments and necklaces which he made
for the ladies.

At last he fashioned a bracelet and a set of rings
more lovely than had ever been seen, and took

them to the Princess Rinda as a gift, asking for
her love in return.

But Rinda was filled with fury. She hurled the
priceless gifts on the floor and struck Rosstheow
the Goldsmith across the face, crying:

'No man can win my love, and none can buy
my favours!'

Nothing daunted, for he knew how important it
was that Vali should be born, Odin left Ruthenia
once more – only to return in changed shape, this
time as a young and handsome warrior. Never
was a fairer man seen: yet he had one blemish,
which even the Allfather of the Æsir could not
rectify: he lacked one eye.

He began to woo the Princess as a young man
should, doing deeds of prowess and valour for
her, bringing her rich gifts, and singing new,
sweet songs of his love for her.

Then it seemed that Rinda relented towards
him; for one day as he ended a new song and knelt
before her, she whispered,

'Come to me this night if you would talk with
me. But you must keep it secret, for none must
know of our love.'

So at dead of night Odin, still in the form of a
young man, stole through the silent palace and
came at last where Billing's sun-white daughter
lay sleeping in her bed. But her hound was tied
up beside her, and when it saw Odin it bayed
loudly, so that she sprang up and called for help;
and at once the whole household, who had been

but feigning sleep, came rushing to her room waving swords and torches.

At last Odin was fairly roused, and he knew that kind words and an honest wooing would not win the headstrong Rinda.

As the soldiers of King Billing reached the door, Rinda struck at him and shrieked aloud that there was a robber in her room, but he drew his magic Rune stick from under his robe and touched her lightly on breast and brow with it. At once she fell back into the arms of those who had come to her rescue stiff and rigid as if dead; and Odin himself sprang behind the bed-hangings and was gone by the time her men reached them.

When Rinda recovered from her swoon, King Billing realized to his dismay that his daughter was mad; and very soon she became so ill that she could hardly stir from her rooms.

About this time a wise woman named Vecha arrived at the palace and offered her services, saying that she was skilled in medicine and could cure even madness. King Billing at once appointed her to attend upon the Princess Rinda, and after giving her foot-baths and soothing drinks which seemed to help her wonderfully, Vecha said:

'My lord King, a violent madness needs a violent cure; also I must be alone with my patient and no sound must disturb her while I am at work. So if you would see your daughter freed from her malady, you must leave me with her from sunset to sunrise, and give orders to all in the palace that no one is to come near her bed-chamber during that time.'

'It shall all be as you advise,' said King Billing, and so he instructed all his household.

Then, as night was falling, Vecha made her solitary way to the shadowy chamber where the sun-white Princess Rinda lay sleeping peacefully. There Vecha flung off the disguise and stood forth as Odin the Allfather, kindly but terrible in his majesty.

With his Rune stick he woke Rinda, and as she woke the madness passed from her and sat up slowly and knew who it was who stood before her.

'Princess Rinda,' said Odin in his slow gentle voice, 'you have always wished to be one of my Battle Maidens, my Valkyries, who ride the storm behind me and go forth to choose those who shall fall in battle and come to swell my host of heroes in Valhalla against the Day of Ragnarok. That cannot be, for you are set aside by the Norns for a fate far higher. You alone among mortal women of Midgard are fated to be the mother of one – the youngest – of the Æsir. Vali shall your son be named, and he shall avenge the death of Baldur the beautiful before he takes his place in Asgard. Nor shall he perish in the Last Great Battle where gods and men shall fall!'

Then the Princess Rinda bowed her head in submission, and when she looked up her eyes were filled with joy at the greatness of the honour which was to be hers. And now she no longer held back when once more Odin asked her to be his wife.

It was not long, however, before Odin bade farewell to his mortal wife Rinda, and returned to Asgard where his true wife Queen Frigga awaited him, and welcomed him without jealousy, for she knew of the decrees of fate.

So the Æsir dwelt as of old in Asgard: but still Hodur went unpunished for the fatal throw of the dart which slew Baldur. Still he ventured out from Breidablik only after dark, for day and night were alike to him, being blind, and wandered in the great wood on the Plains of Ida until the first cry of the birds told him that morning was coming.

Now too he carried on his arm the Shield of Darkness which Mimring the Troll of the Forest had made for him, and also a magic sword which all might fear to meet on a dark night. Yet still, as he wandered, he wept for the death of his beloved brother and for the sad fate which was his.

Then one day as Heimdall stood on guard at the Gate of Asgard, there came walking up the Bridge Bifrost a little child carrying a bow and a quiver of arrows.

'No child with uncombed hair and unwashed hands passes this way into Asgard!' cried Heimdall.

'Bring me before Odin the Allfather where he sits in Valhalla!' replied the child in a voice so strange that Heimdall obeyed without a thought of questioning it.

They came to Valhalla, and there Hermodur challenged them:

'No child with uncombed hair and unwashed hands passes this way into Valhalla!' he cried. 'No man from Midgard may enter who shows no wound nor stain of blood upon him to prove that he died in battle!'

'Bring me before Odin my father,' answered the child; and his voice was already fuller than when he had first spoken to Heimdall. Even as the Warder of Bifrost had done, the Guardian of Valhalla did not question the imperious voice of the wonderful child. He stood aside, and the boy strode straight up the centre of Valhalla, while the Æsir stared, and the Einheriar, the Heroes, marvelled, until he stood before the throne.

'Welcome!' cried Odin rising to his feet. 'This is Vali, my son and the Princess Rinda's. This is he who was born to perform the holy work of vengeance for Baldur's death.'

'But how can this boy overcome strong Hodur with his Shield of Darkness and his Sword of Terror?' asked the Æsir.

'It is true that I am but one night old,' answered Vali, 'yet ere this night is passed I shall be fully grown; and even as tender Spring grows and overcomes mighty Winter, so shall I slay Hodur.'

Then, while all marvelled at his wondrous growth, for he grew from a boy into a youth and from a youth into a man even as they watched

him, Vali passed on through the hall of Valhalla
and out into the dark woods beyond.

There Hodur wandered, desperate and desolate,
hate growing in his heart which had known only
love. And suddenly he heard a clear voice crying
aloud:

'Slayer of Baldur, your hour has come! Have a
care to yourself, for the avenger is here!'

Desperately Hodur raised the Shield of Darkness in front of him and rushed towards the sound
of the voice, waving the Sword of Terror in his
hand. An arrow tore through the darkness – a
second – and a third, and Hodur sank to the
ground and died.

Then Vali's shout of triumph echoed through
all Asgard, and as the Æsir hastened to the spot
where the dead Hodur lay, they found him a great
and shining warrior standing above the body of
Baldur's slayer.

But down in Hela's dismal land Hodur passed
with bent head over the Gioll Bridge and stood in
the shadowy hall, sad and alone.

Then Baldur rose from his place at the table
and came to greet him with open arms and a smile
of welcome and forgiveness on his face.

'Greetings, dear brother!' he cried. 'Now that
you are come, Helheim has lost half its sorrows
. . . It was not you but evil Loki who caused my
death – yet I can hardly regret that your hand
held the fatal mistletoe, since otherwise you would
not have come to join me here in my loneliness.

Now you and I are together again, and we may pass our time without sadness, until the Day of Ragnarok when it is fated that we shall see the light again.'

14

THE PUNISHMENT OF LOKI

Although Odin seldom smiled now, and Frigga wept often as she sat weaving the clouds in Fensalir, life in Asgard continued for the Æsir much as before the death of Baldur. The shadow of Ragnarok had drawn nearer and hung over them, dark and terrible: but the nightly feast in Valhalla was as joyous as ever; and upon Midgard wars waxed and were waged, the Valkyries rode to more and more battles, and the host of the Einheriar, the Chosen Heroes, grew apace.

Baldur and Hodur sat no more among the Æsir,

and though Vali was now one of them, another face was missing – Loki's.

Since the death of Baldur he had not ventured to Asgard. Although no vengeance had been meted out to him, he knew that it must come. Odin could not be ignorant that his hand had shaped the fatal dart of mistletoe and guided Hodur's hand. Moreover the Æsir must also know that it was he in the likeness of the Giantess Thokk who had refused to weep Baldur out of Helheim.

But as the time passed and no hand was raised against him, Loki grew tired of stirring up evil in Midgard; and he also began to feel slighted and neglected. It was as if the Æsir had forgotten all about him: and yet surely he, Loki, was as great as any of them, and had done a deed which no one else in all the Nine Worlds would have dared.

So when the next Festival of Harvest came round, though Loki had not the effrontery to present himself in Asgard, and knew well that his old enemy Heimdall would never allow him to cross the Bifrost Bridge, he set out for Ægir's halls on the island in the Kattigat.

Here all the Æsir were feasting as they had done each year since Thor had brought the great brewing kettle: but Thor himself, as Loki well knew, was away in Jotunheim where the Giants were beginning to stir again and plot evil against gods and men.

At the door of the hall Loki found Eldir, who was Ægir's cook.

'Tell me, Eldir,' he said, 'what are the Æsir talking about as they sit around Ægir's banquet board?'

'They are talking of their weapons and their deeds of war,' answered Eldir. 'Of all those within, both Æsir and Vanir, not one speaks a good word of you.'

'Then I shall go in and take my place among them,' said Loki. 'I can at least bring them bitter spice for their drink and mingle venom with their mead!'

'Be sure that if you pour slander and foul words on the Æsir, they will wipe it off on you,' warned Eldir.

But Loki replied scornfully: 'You talk too much, but you can never out-talk me, for I have an answer to everything!' and with that he pushed past him into the hall.

When Loki appeared, silence fell upon all the Æsir, and they sat looking with loathing and contempt upon their evil and unwelcome visitor.

'I arrive here thirsty and tired after a long journey,' cried Loki impudently, 'and not one of the Æsir so much as offers me a drink of the good mead. Why do you all sit silent? Will you not at least ask me to sit at your table?'

'The Æsir will never again give you a seat at their banquet,' said Bragi. 'For they know well what you have done – and what you deserve.'

'Odin, do you not remember your oath?' cried Loki, turning to the Allfather. 'In the morning of time we blended our blood together, and you vowed never to refuse me a share of any cup of ale that you raised to your lips.'

'That is true,' answered Odin quietly. 'Therefore, Vidar my son, move up so that the Father of the Fenris Wolf may sit. Never let it be said that the Æsir forgot an oath.'

Loki seated himself and took a long pull at the meadcup. But he could no longer control his evil tongue, and the hate and jealousy within him welled up until he could contain himself no longer.

'Greetings to you, mighty Æsir!' he cried. 'I greet you all, except cowardly Bragi who would have kept me away from my rightful place among you.'

'I will give you out of my store a steed and a sword: yes, and rings too,' said Bragi in an undertone, 'if only you will cease abusing the Æsir: if only you will keep the peace at this solemn feast.'

'Bragi you coward!' shouted Loki. 'You never fought in a battle, nor used sword or horse. No, you were hiding in case a stray arrow should find you!'

'Be sure if we were outside, and not guests at Ægir's feast, I would have your severed head in my hand before many minutes were passed,' said Bragi hotly.

'I pray you, for the sake of our love, do not provoke Loki now!' whispered the fair Iduna laying one hand on her husband's arm and the other on Loki's shoulder.

'Hold your peace, Iduna,' said Loki. 'I think

you the most evil-minded of women thus to touch
me who slew your husband's brother.'

'I do but try to keep the peace,' sobbed Iduna,
'for I would not see you and Bragi come to blows
here in Ægir's hall.'

'Surely you are drunk or mad to behave thus,
Loki,' cried Odin. 'Therefore speak no more,
unless you speak words of peace.'

'It is you, Odin, who should be ashamed to
interfere between warriors,' shouted Loki. 'Everyone knows that you have often given the victory
in battle to cowards and shaken Gungnir over the
heads of men braver than yourself. Moreover you
played the coward yourself in the island of
Samsey, turning yourself into a witch and doing
the vile things that witches do!'

'You should not speak of ancient things done at
the beginning of the world when you and Odin
were as brothers,' said Queen Frigga hastily,
trying to keep the peace.

'Keep quiet, Frigga the faithless,' screamed
Loki. 'We all know that you were the lover of Vili
and Ve while their brother Odin was away!'

This was so absurd a thing to say about Frigga,
the goddess of married love and faith, that all the
Æsir laughed, though Frigga cried:

'If only my son Baldur were here, you would
not dare to insult me so!'

'Baldur will never sit at your feasts again,'
taunted Loki, 'for I caused his death, and kept
him in Helheim!'

'Hold your peace, you drunken braggart,' cried Freya angrily. 'You are no man, but a mere half-woman!'

'Filthy witch-hag!' gasped Loki, for Freya's words were the most unforgivable insult that could ever be spoken in the North. 'There is not one of the Æsir who has not been your lover; and I know well what you did with the Dwarfs to win the Brisingamen!'

Now more than one of the Æsir clapped hand to sword and made ready to fall upon Loki. But at a sign from Odin they sat back and were silent.

After a few minutes Loki, who could not bear to be ignored, began again:

'Ha, there I see my friend Tyr!' he cried. 'Tyr the war-lord! A poor war-lord with only one hand! My sweet son Fenris Wolf bit it off.'

'The Wolf lies bound at the world's end,' said Frey quietly. 'Unless you are careful of your words, Loki, it will be your turn next to feel our chains about you.'

'And who are you to gibe at my son Fenris?' cried Loki. 'You who bought a woman, Gymir's daughter, with your sword. When Fenris comes against you at Ragnarok he will make an easy meal of a warrior who has lost his sword.'

'You are drunk, Loki, and out of your wits,' said Heimdall quietly. 'Go outside now as a decent drinker should. We babble nonsense in our cups, and our words are soon forgotten – if we stop in time.'

'So you have come to the banquet, shivering servant of the Æsir,' sneered Loki. 'You are tired, I suppose, of standing in the rain on Bifrost Bridge with never a wink of sleep!'

Then Skadi spoke in a cold, faraway voice, the gift of the seeress coming upon her so that for a moment she could see into the future:

'Loki the dog!' she said. 'Loki the dog! Not long shall he go free with his tail wagging! I see him bound upon sword-sharp rocks by the Æsir – fettered by wolf-sinews, fettered by iron, fettered by his own son!'

'And does Skadi, the Giant's daughter, deign to speak to me!' cried Loki. 'She forgets that I was the foremost at the slaughter of her father Thiassi ... She only remembers that she was once my lover!'

'Now drink this goblet of old mead, and cease from this senseless talk and these untrue tales,' said the golden-haired Sif gently, making a final attempt to keep the peace of the banquet. 'Drink, and cease from reviling the Æsir.'

But Loki was past all reason now:

'And here is Sif!' he cried. 'Sif whose hair I once took! Even she proved unfaithful to her husband and held me in her arms instead!'

Even as he spoke there came a rumble of thunder; the earth shook, and Thor himself strode into the hall, his red beard bristling and sparking with anger.

'Hold your peace, vile creature!' he roared.

'Miolnir, my mighty hammer, shall cut short your speech if you utter another lying word.'

'Ha, the son of dirt at last!' sneered Loki, edging his way towards the door none the less. 'You threaten now, mighty Thor: but you will change your tune when you meet my Fenris Wolf at Ragnarok!'

'That is as the Norns shall decide,' answered Thor. 'But speak again and I will fling you into the uttermost Arctic where none shall see you more.'

'Never speak of journeys into Jotunheim!' scoffed Loki. 'We all know how you hid in the thumb of Skrymir's glove. And as for flinging me, we know also that even Skrymir's wallet was so tightly laced that you could not undo the straps, and were forced to go without your supper.'

'The hammer that killed Rungnir shall kill you also!' roared Thor, whirling up Miolnir, 'and you shall go to Nastrond and boil in Hvengelmir as food for the Nid Hog!'

'I have only spoken the truth, but I will go now,' shouted Loki. 'I know of old that Thor cannot keep his temper! . . . As for Ægir's hall, I hope it burns with fire before another year is over!'

With that he departed; but the Æsir, now roused to great anger, held council there and then, and swore never to rest until Loki was caught and bound. So, when the feast was ended, they went out over the world in search of him.

Loki knew well that the Æsir would never forgive what he had done, nor leave him to work
more evil; so he set about finding a safe hiding-
place.

After wandering through Midgard for some
time he decided on a certain lofty mountain from
which he could see for many miles in every direction. Here he built himself a house with four
doors beside the Frananger Falls; and he would
often turn himself into a salmon and hide in the
deep river or behind the arch of the falling water.

'They can never catch me here!' he cried boast-
fully as he sat one day by the fire in his house,
keeping a wary lookout through all his doors. 'I
could see them coming far away, change myself
into a salmon, and hide so well in the Frananger
Falls or away down the river that none of them
would find me ... If they borrowed Ran's net
they might catch me, even as I caught Andvari
the Dwarf. But Ran is my friend: we both delight
in working evil – and she will never lend her net
... As for the Æsir, they will never think of
making one. And even if they did, none of them
have the skill to do it. Even *I* would find it
difficult; but of course there is nothing that I
cannot do! I suppose I would begin like this . . .'

He took up a length of twine and began knitting
and tying it cunningly into the meshes of a net.
Happening to look up after a little while, he saw a
band of the Æsir, headed by Thor, coming up the
mountain in the distance.

With a curse he flung the half-made net into the fire, slipped out of the further door and, turning himself into a salmon, slid out of sight into the river and hid under the Frananger Falls.

When the Æsir arrived at the house there was no sign of Loki, nor could they discover him anywhere nearby.

'This is where he was, however,' insisted Thor. 'For father Odin saw him here when he looked out from Lidskialf over all the worlds. Loki was sitting in this house beside the waterfall.'

The mention of the waterfall seemed to remind Honir of something, and he turned back into the house and looked long and carefully at the fire.

'See,' he said quietly, 'those ashes form part of a net such as Ran uses to draw sailors down under the sea.

'Now I remember once on a time how Odin and Loki and I went forth into Midgard, and Loki caught the Dwarf Andvari with Ran's net when the Dwarf had turned himself into a fish and hidden under just such a waterfall as this . . . It seems to me that Loki must be hiding under the Frananger Falls in the shape of a fish, and before we came he was trying to see if it were possible to make a net. For he knows well that Ran will never lend hers to catch one of the Giant kin. So let us see if we can make such a net ourselves, and fish for Loki!'

The Æsir at once set to work, using the shape in the ashes as a model, and very soon they had a net long enough to draw the river in one sweep.

Then Thor took one end and all the rest of the Æsir the other, and they drew it through the water of the river and through the falls. But Loki darted away in front of it and hid between two stones: however, he touched the net in passing, and the Æsir knew that something was there.

So they weighted the net so that nothing could pass under it, and drew it once again from the falls right down-stream until they came near the sea. And when Loki saw the great ocean where no salmon could live, he was afraid and leapt suddenly over the net, and sped back upstream to hide once more under the Frananger Falls.

But they had seen him, and once more they prepared to draw the river. But this time half the Æsir were at each end of the net and Thor waded along in mid-stream just behind it. So they went down again toward the sea, and presently Loki realized that he had only two chances of escape: either to leap back over the net, hoping that Thor would miss him, or else to dare the dangers of the sea.

At the last moment he was afraid, for he knew that Ægir, Lord of the Sea, would have many a monster waiting there for him. So he leapt suddenly back over the net.

But Thor saw him and with a shout seized him by the tail and held tight, squeezing so hard that salmon have narrow tails to this day.

Now Loki took his own form again; and as he had been captured outside Asgard and in no place where the laws of hospitality protected him, he knew that he could expect nothing but his just punishment from the Æsir for the murder of Baldur the beautiful.

They dragged him away to a cave far below the world of men, and there they set three sharp slabs of stone on edge and bound Loki upon them. And one stone was under his shoulders, one under his thighs and one under the calves of his legs.

To find fetters that would hold him the Æsir turned Loki's evil son Ali into a wolf, and he at once killed his brother Narfi and tore him to pieces. Out of Narfi's sinews they made thongs with which they bound Loki, drawing the fetters through a hole which they made in each of the three stones. And then by magic they turned the sinews into iron.

To complete the punishment of Loki the Evil One, Skadi took a venomous serpent and hung it above his head so that the poison dripped upon him and he writhed in pain.

But even Loki was not without one person in all the world to love him, and that was his faithful wife, the Giantess called Sigyn. She came hastening to his side and held a cup to catch the drips of venom. But when the cup was full she had to turn away to empty it; and every time she did so Loki writhed in pain as the venom fell on his face, and the whole earth shook and trembled.

Only once did a man of Midgard find his way to the cavern where Loki lay waiting for Ragnarok, and that man was Thorkill the great traveller. Through a sunless land he sailed where no stars shone at night and there was deep gloom at midday; and at last the fuel grew short so that he and his crew were forced to eat their meat raw. Then a plague smote them so that many died; and at length when hope seemed dead they saw a fire at a great distance and in time came to a cave of the sea where two Giants sat cooking fish.

With a jewel set at his mast-head to reflect the light, Thorkill sailed past them, after bandying riddles which he was quick-witted enough to answer, and he came to the unsailed, untrodden regions beyond the world.

Here he landed in the deep gloom and set out with his companions until they came to a rock of an enormous size; and there he caused his men to make a fire by striking flint stones and iron together, and saw the entrance to a cavern.

Through the narrow cleft in the rock he went, his men bearing torches before and behind him, and they picked their way among gliding, glistening serpents. Next he crossed a sluggish stream of black water, and came to a place where, in a foul and gloomy cavern, Loki lay bound upon his three rocks.

It seemed to them that he was a huge and terrible Giant, held by mighty chains, with the hairs standing out on his head like twigs of dogwood. When they put up their hands to draw out one of these hairs as proof that Loki indeed lived, he moved in his bonds, and immediately the black venom of the great snake began to drip from the roof above.

In terror Thorkill and his men covered themselves in their cloaks and turned to steal away from that dreadful cavern. But only five of them came out of it unhurt. For one man peeping out from under his cloak, the poison touched his head, which it took off at the neck as if it had been severed with a sword. Another glanced from beneath his hand, and was immediately blinded; and a third, putting forth his hand to save himself from falling, lost his whole arm on the instant.

Thorkill and the survivors struggled back to their ship, and sailed away through the darkness for weeks and weeks. They were wrecked on the homeward voyage, and only Thorkill lived to tell the tale of how he had seen Loki, the Evil One, chained to his three rocks under the northern parts of the world.

And there Loki lies, bound with bonds that cannot be broken until Ragnarok, when he shall be loosed to fight against the Æsir on the Day of the Last Great Battle.

15

RAGNAROK

Even from the morning of time Odin had known, the
Æsir soon knew, and even the dwellers in Midgard
learnt to know also, that the whole world would
perish on a day – the Day of Ragnarok, the Twilight
of the Gods – the Day of the Last Great Battle.

Baldur was dead and Hodur was dead also.
Loki was bound, and Valhalla was growing full of
the Einheriar. There were shadows over Asgard,
and in Jotunheim the Giants stirred and muttered
threateningly. In Midgard men turned towards
the evil Loki had taught them, treachery grew and
greed and pride also.

Odin knew much of what was to happen when Ragnarok came: but there was much he did not know, for even he could not see the future. If the Norns knew, they would not speak: their task was to weave the web of each man's life, but not the life of the whole world.

But here and there a strange woman was born or died who could see into the future, some a little way and concerning little things; but one or two with powers of sight beyond that of any other creature. Such a one was the dead Volva whom Odin had raised from her grave to tell him of the death of Baldur. Such another was born and lived her life in Midgard. Her name was Haid and she was famed among men for her prophecies.

Seated in Lidskialf, whence he could see all that happened in the Nine Worlds, Odin saw Haid, the wise sibyl, passing from house to house among men. And suddenly he knew that here was one wiser even than Volva, one who could answer what he desired most to know.

So he went down to Midgard wearing his usual disguise of wide-brimmed hat, blue cloak, and tall staff. Before he went in search of Haid, the Valkyries had visited her, bringing such gifts as the high ones of Asgard could give: cunning treasure-spells, rune sticks, and rods of divination.

Odin came to her as she sat alone before a cave overlooking the broad land of the Danes and the blue waters of the Sound. He came as a man, bringing her presents of rings and necklaces, and begging her to read the future for him. But she knew him at once and spoke to him in the deep, thrilling tones of a prophetess:

'What ask you of me? Why would you tempt me? I know all, Odin: yes, I know where you have hidden your eye in the holy well of Mimir. I can see all things: both the world's beginning and the world's ending. I can see Ginnungagap as it was before the Sons of Borr raised the earth out of it: the Giant Ymir I know, and the Cow Audumla . . . I can see the shaft of death, the mistletoe that Loki cut from the oak; the dart that flew into Baldur's heart, and Frigga weeping in Fensalir.'

'You know of the past, and that I know also,' said Odin. 'But, since the gift is yours and yours alone, look into the future, wise Haid – you whom we in Asgard call Vola, the Sibyl – look and tell me of the World's Ending: tell me of Ragnarok and the Great Battle on the Plain of Vigrid.'

Then he took his stand behind Haid the Vola, placing his hands above her head and murmuring the runes of wisdom so that his knowledge should be mingled with hers.

And now her eyes grew wide and vacant as she gazed out across the land and over the water, seeing neither: seeing things unseen.

'There shall come the Fimbul Winter,' she cried, 'after man's evil has reached its height. For brother shall slay brother, and son shall not spare father, and honour shall be dead among men.

'In that awful Winter snow shall drive from all quarters, frost shall not break, the winds shall be keen, and the sun give no heat. And for three years shall that Fimbul Winter last.

'Eastward in Iron Wood an aged witch is sitting, breeding the brood of Fenris and the wolf that shall swallow the Sun. He shall feed on the lives of death-doomed mortals, spattering the heavens with their red blood.

'Ragnarok comes: I see it far in the days to be. Yet to me, the far-seer, it is as if that day were now, and all that I see in the future is happening before me now. I see it, and I tell you what I see and hear as it rises about me until Future and Present seem as one.

'For I see the Wolf Skoll who in that far day swallows the Sun, and the Moon is swallowed also, while the stars are quenched with blood. Now the earth shakes, the trees and the rocks are torn up and all things fall to ruin.

'Away in Jotunheim the red cock Fialar crows loudly; and another cock with golden crest crows over Asgard. Then all bonds are loosened: the Fenris Wolf breaks free; the sea gushes over the land as Jormungand the Midgard Serpent swims ashore. Then the ship Naglfar is loosened: it is made of dead men's nails – therefore when a man dies, shear his nails close so that Naglfar may be long in the building. But now I see it moving over the flood, and the Giant Hymir steers it. Fenris advances with open mouth, and Jormungand blows venom over sea and air: terrible is he as he takes his place beside the Wolf Fenris.

'Then the sky splits open and the Sons of Muspell come in fire: Surtur leads them with his flaming sword, and when they ride over Bifrost the bridge breaks behind them and falls in pieces to the earth. Loki also is set free and comes to the Field of Vigrid; he and Hymir lead the Frost Giants to the battle. But all Hela's champions follow Loki: Garm the Hell Hound bays fiercely before the Gnipa Cave, and his jaws slobber with blood.

'Now I hear Heimdall in the Gate of Asgard blowing upon the Giallar Horn. Its notes sound clear and shrill throughout all worlds: it is the Day of Ragnarok. The Æsir meet together; Odin rides to Mimir's Well for the last time. Yggdrasill the World Tree trembles, and nothing shall be without fear in heaven or in earth.

'Now I see the Æsir put on their armour and ride to the field of battle. Odin rides first in his golden helmet and his fair armour; Sleipnir is beneath him and he holds the spear Gungnir in his hand. He rides against the Fenris Wolf, and Thor stands at his side, shaking Miolnir: yet he cannot help Odin, for all his strength is needed in his own battle with Jormungand.

'Now Frey fights against Surtur; the struggle is long, but Frey falls at the last. Ah, he would not have died had he his sword in his hand: but that sword he gave to Skirnir. Oh, how loudly Garm bays in the Gnipa Cave! Now he has broken loose and fights against Tyr: had Tyr two hands it would go hard with Garm, but now they slay and are slain the one by the other.

'Thor slays the Midgard Serpent, and no greater deed was ever done. He strides away from the spot; nine paces only, and then he falls to the earth and dies, so deadly is the venom which Jormungand has poured upon him.

'Odin and Fenris still fight together: but in the end the Wolf has the victory and devours Odin. But Vidar strides forward to avenge his father, and sets his foot on the lower jaw of Fenris. On that foot is the shoe made of the scraps of leather which men cut from their toes or heels: therefore should men cut often and fling away if they desire to help the Æsir. Vidar takes the Wolf by the upper jaw and tears him apart, and that is the end of Fenris.

'Loki battles with Heimdall, and in their last struggle each slays the other and both fall.

'Now Surtur spreads fire over the whole earth and all things perish. Darkness descends, and I can see no more.'

The voice of Haid the Vola faded away into silence. But still she sat rigid and still gazing beyond the distance, gazing into the future with wide, unseeing eyes.

Very slowly, as he stood behind her, it seemed to Odin that her power was creeping into him. His own eye grew misty – grew dark – and then on a sudden he was looking out with two eyes, with her eyes and not his own.

At first he saw only a great waste of water, tossing and tumbling over all the world. But as he watched, a new earth rose out of the sea, green and fruitful, with unfading forests and pleasant meadows smiling in the light of a new sun. Then the waters fell away, making wide rivers, and sparkling falls and a new blue sea about the land.

Then, on Ida's Plain where Asgard had stood before, he saw Vidar and Vali, the two of the Æsir who had survived through Ragnarok. Thor's two sons, Magni and Modi, came to join them, bearing Miolnir in their hands. After this the earth opened and back from Helheim came Baldur the Beautiful, holding his brother Hodur by the hand.

They sat down and spoke together concerning all that had happened, of the passing of Fenris and Jormungand, and other evils. Then, shining among the grass and flowers, they saw the ancient golden chessmen of the Æsir, and collecting them began to play once more on the board of life.

Presently Honir came to them out of Vanaheim, bringing great wisdom to the new Æsir. At his bidding new halls rose on Ida's Plain, glittering palaces waiting for the souls of dead men and women from Midgard.

For in Midgard also life came again. In the deep place called Hoddminir's Holt a man and a woman had escaped from Surtur's fire. Now they awoke from sleep, Lif and Lifthrasir; and for food they found the morning dew was all they needed. From them were born many children so that Midgard was peopled anew. And there were children also in the new Asgard which was called Gimli the Gem Lea, where the halls were thatched with gold. There the blessed among men mingled with the new race of the Æsir, and the new Sun shone brightly, and the new world was filled with light and song.

Then Odin wept with joy, and as the tears coursed down his face, the vision faded into the greyness of the cold Northern world where Ragnarok is yet to come. The wind moaned over the chill plains, the wolves howled in the lonely mountains, and across the sea stole forth a longship hung with shields in which Viking men went out to harry and slay and burn.

The old sibyl sat alone by her cave, chanting the words of the *Volo-spa*, the poem of prophecy, the finest of all the old Northern poems which are still known among men.

But Odin threaded his way quietly across Midgard to Bifrost Bridge, up its gleaming arch where Heimdall stood on guard, and so brought his good news to the Æsir.

For now he knew the meaning of the mysterious word which he had whispered into Baldur's ear as his dead son lay upon the funeral ship: the word 'Rebirth' which was to bring comfort and hope to the Men of Midgard as well as to the Gods of Asgard.

TALES OF THE GREEK HEROES
Roger Lancelyn Green

Some of the oldest and most famous stories in the world – the adventures of Perseus, the labours of Heracles, the voyage of Jason and the Argonauts – are vividly retold in this single, connected narrative of the Heroic Age, from the coming of the Immortals to the first fall of Troy. With fresh dialogue and a brisk pace, the myths of this version are enthrallingly vivid.

THE WIZARD OF OZ
L. Frank Baum

When a cyclone hits her Kansas home, Dorothy and her dog Toto are whisked to the magical land of Oz. To find her way back to Kansas, she must follow the yellow brick road to the City of Emeralds where the great Wizard lives. But first Dorothy, Toto and their companions the Tin Woodman, Scarecrow and Cowardly Lion have many adventures on their strange and sometimes frightening journey.

THE RED BADGE OF COURAGE
Stephen Crane

Young Henry Fleming had always dreamt of performing heroic deeds in battle. But the reality, as a raw recruit in the American Civil War, is a mental and physical torment. And as Henry fights his inner battles with fear, self-doubt, trauma and vainglory throughout his first harrowing action, he has no idea whether war will make him a coward, a hero – or a man.

THROUGH THE LOOKING GLASS
Lewis Carroll

When Alice steps through the looking glass, she enters a world of chess pieces and nursery rhyme characters who behave very oddly. Humpty Dumpty, the Lion and the Unicorn, Tweedledum and Tweedledee, the dotty White Knight and the sharp-tempered Red Queen – none of them are straightforward. In fact, through the looking glass everything is 'contrariwise'.

MOONFLEET
J. Meade Falkner

Everyone in the tiny village of Moonfleet lives by the sea one way or another, so it's no surprise when young John Trenchard gets involved in the smuggling trade. Forced to flee England with a price on his head, John little guesses the adventures and trials he will face before he sees Moonfleet again – or the change in his fortunes when he does.

LITTLE WOMEN
Louisa M. Alcott

The good-natured March girls – Meg, Jo, Beth and Amy – manage to lead interesting lives despite Father's absence at war and the family's lack of money. Whether they're making plans for putting on a play or forming a secret society, their gaiety is infectious and even Laurie next door is swept up in their enthusiasm. Written from Louisa May Alcott's own experiences, this is a remarkable story.

HEIDI
Johanna Spyri

Heidi is five when she is sent to live with her grandfather in his lonely hut high in the Alps. She quickly grows to love her carefree new life with him in the mountain air, and the old man comes to love her too. They are both unhappy when Heidi is sent away again, to a family in town, but she soon manages to get home to her Alps – and to share her happiness with her new friends.

OLIVER TWIST
Charles Dickens

Until he is nine, Oliver spends his life in a workhouse orphanage where he becomes notorious for daring to ask for more food. When he runs away to London, he falls into the company of a gang of pickpockets including Fagin, Bill Sikes and the Artful Dodger. Oliver's future looks uncertain, until a mysterious plot against him is unravelled by the kind Mr Brownlow.